FORBIDDEN BILLIONAIRE

IT'S COMPLICATED - BOOK FOUR

MAGGIE COLE

PULSE PRESS INC

For anyone who is struggling to find their happily ever after, this one is for you!

Because life is sometimes not black and white—it's complicated.

XOXO

Maggie Cole

PROLOGUE

Fifteen Years Ago

Innocence is at the root of my mistake. Fear is the branch that continues to grow and thrive, keeping me locked into my fallacy.

It's already been a long day. I'm walking up the stairs to my apartment floor and about to open the door to leave the stairwell when I hear the sobs.

I look behind me, but no one is there.

"It'll be okay," a female voice says.

Just go to your apartment and stay out of it.

"My life is over," she says in her Colombian accent.

Shit, that's Valeria.

I'm a sucker. I've always been. A woman crying is the worst sound on earth for me. Instead of staying out of it, I butt right in.

1

I walk up the stairs. Sure enough, Valeria and her roommate Mary are there.

"Valeria, what's wrong?"

Her tear-filled eyes stab me in the heart. "I have to go back to Colombia."

"What? Why?"

"My student visa ran out, and I haven't been able to get a job that will get me a work visa."

"What? Surely there is something you can do."

"There isn't. The only way I can stay in the country without marrying a United States citizen is by getting a work visa." She starts to sob again and puts her head between her knees.

That's not fair.

Mary rubs her back, helpless.

I sit on the step right below Valeria and realize she's clutching a piece of paper. "Can I see that?"

Valeria hands me the paper.

It's from the United States immigration office. I read it, and my heart drops. "This says you need to leave in the next week?"

"I've been here since I was fourteen and in high school. I don't want to go back to Colombia. My father will make me marry one of his men, and I won't be able to pursue my acting career. I don't want that life."

I do the math in my head. "You've been here for six years?"

"Yes."

Six years, and they are making her go back? She'll be forced into a marriage?

"There has to be something we can do," I tell her. I've known Valeria for the last two years. I moved into this building when I was eighteen. We are part of a group of tenants who get together often for parties, as we are all around the same age.

"There isn't. My life is over," she sobs again.

"Maybe we can find someone to marry you," Mary suggests.

Valeria head snaps. "I just said I don't want to get married."

"Yeah, to one of your father's men. Get married to a citizen to keep your status."

"And who's going to do that, Mary?" Valeria asks.

Mary addresses me. "Jamison, you could marry Valeria."

My pulse increases.

"Mary, don't be ridiculous. This isn't Jamison's problem."

My mouth goes dry. I stare at Valeria.

I could marry her, and then she wouldn't be forced to get married back in Colombia.

"You wouldn't have to stay married forever," Mary states.

"How long would we have to be married?" I ask.

"You're not considering this?" Valeria furrows her brows.

I shrug. "I don't know. It's just a piece of paper, and it doesn't seem fair for you to have to ruin your life over a technicality."

"You would do that? You would get married?" Valeria asks.

"I wasn't exactly looking for a wife this morning when I woke up, but I don't see the big deal. If we don't have to stay married forever and it solves your problem, then what's the issue? If I can't help a friend out, then what kind of friend am I?"

"See? I knew we could come up with a solution!" Mary hugs Valeria.

"We would have to live together," Valeria says.

"I'll kick Chase out. He's talking about buying a house anyway."

"Really?"

"Yes. You can have his room and do whatever you want to do. I'll do the same. You get to stay in the country, and I get to help out a friend. Win-win."

Mary claps. "This is perfect! Can I be your maid of honor?"

Valeria frowns. "This isn't a real marriage. We aren't going to have a big white wedding with a reception."

I wink at Valeria. "You can wear white if you want."

Valeria's face gets red. "No offense, but you aren't really my type."

She is definitely not my type, either. Valeria is beautiful and kind, but there is no chemistry between us. I also know Valeria is a lesbian. Most guys make the mistake that she's straight, but she's not the least interested. She wants no part of what I can offer her. It's another reason she shouldn't be marrying anyone her father picks.

"What's so funny? You can't expect her to sleep with you," Mary accuses me.

"I have no plans of sleeping with you, Valeria, or attempting to. If I kissed you, I'd feel like I was kissing my sister. This marriage will be strictly in the friend zone. You can date whoever you want. I will date whoever I want," I assure her.

Valeria smiles. "So you will marry me, lie to the government, and we both can live how we want to?"

"Why not? It's not going to change my life at all."

And that's what I had all wrong.

Quinn

Present Day

"ARE YOU ABLE TO GET THE PENTHOUSE STILL?" I ASK VIVIAN. Chase has been shot, and he was supposed to sign for it earlier that day.

"Hopefully."

I hear his voice.

"Oh my God, Vivian, your face!"

"I'm okay."

"How is he?" Jamison's voice is full of worry.

"He's recovering. He'll be okay," Vivian tells him.

He turns to me and relief replaces his worry. "You doing okay?"

Don't break down, Quinn. This is not the time. You need to forget about him and move on. Don't give him any further reason to talk to you.

"Yeah. Glad you had a safe flight." I turn and walk away.

Noah, Piper, Xander, Charlotte, and Vivian's parents are all at the hospital.

I concentrate on all of them, trying to appear interested in their conversation, but the entire time my insides are shaking, and I remind myself to breathe and not focus on Jamison.

I'm playing my role well. I make it through dinner. I sit as far away from him as possible. I engage in conversation with Vivian's mom, hoping it'll be easier not to think about him. I need to pay closer attention to what she says because of her broken English, but having to concentrate on all her words only makes my mind wander more.

"Quinn?" Vivian's mom puts her hand on mine.

"Oh, sorry. I need to go to the restroom. I'll see you all back in the waiting room."

Her mom looks worried. I never could fool her. She always knows when something is wrong with one of us girls.

I don't need to use the restroom, but I do need to breathe. And I can't with Jamison around. All I can think of is how much I want him to wrap me in his arms, and that will never happen again.

Once I get inside the restroom, I see no one else is in it. I put my hands on the countertop and inhale a few times, but the tears flow. Seeing him is ripping my heart out, and I don't know how to stop the bleeding.

I should have locked the door. There are only three stalls, but I should have gone into one or locked the main door. Piper comes in as soon as I start crying.

She rushes over to me and pulls me into her arms. "Quinn, what's going on?"

I shake my head.

"Quinn, I haven't pushed you, but enough is enough. What is going on between you and Jamison?"

"Nothing," I tell her.

It's the truth.

"Quinn. Something is going on. Why won't you tell me?"

I blow my nose and avoid looking at her. The shame of it is too much. I've known Piper forever, and she's my closest friend. I've never kept anything from her until now.

She pushes. "Why are you avoiding Jamison?"

"I don't want to talk about it."

She grabs me by the shoulders. "Quinn. Enough. You're hurt. Tell me what is going on!"

Her brown eyes are blazing into mine, and I can no longer keep this to myself. "We were together."

"Yes, we all figured that."

I take a shaky breath.

"It started in New York?"

"It did."

"What did he do to you?"

What did he do to me? Made me fall in love with him, be the most incredible man I've ever been with, and fail to tell me what he sees as just a small detail in his life that he thinks doesn't affect us.

But you found out a while back, and you still didn't put a stop to it.

I close my eyes and then open them. Piper is still waiting for me to answer her.

Don't tell her. She'll cut his balls off before we even leave the hospital.

"Nothing. It's just not going to work out," I finally say.

"We aren't leaving this bathroom until you tell me."

I'm not getting out of this.

"Okay. Fine. I'll tell you, but you can't go all apeshit crazy."

She squints. "Why would I do that?"

I tilt my head. "Do you really have to ask me that?"

"Fine. I promise I won't go berserk. Now tell me what is going on."

The door opens, and Charlotte walks in. "Didn't know we were having a meeting. Where's my invite?" she teases. "Visiting hours are over, and Chase is stable. The guys are figuring out the home healthcare situation, and then we can all go home."

"That's good," I say.

Charlotte gazes between our faces. "What's going on?"

Before I can stop her, Piper says, "Quinn is finally going to tell us what is going on between her and Jamison."

"Nothing is going on," I blurt out.

"Now it isn't. But it was, and you were just about to tell me why you both look like sad puppy dogs," Piper says.

Charlotte puts her hand on my arm. "Quinn, tell us what is going on."

"We were together," I tell her.

"Yes, we all can see that. Why aren't you now?"

Heat rises to my face. *This is so embarrassing. It sounds so horrible.*

Because it is horrible...it's not right.

Charlotte and Piper are waiting for me to tell them, and there is no way out.

"I promised I wouldn't tell anyone."

"We won't, either. Now, spill it," Charlotte says.

"You both need to remember we are in a hospital, and Chase has been shot. We do not need to cause a scene."

"What did he do?" Piper asks.

"See, that right there is why I don't want to tell you."

She sighs. "Quinn, the clock is ticking. Spill it."

I look to Charlotte for help, but I'm not going to get it.

How do I even tell them this? Ugh. This is going to sound so bad.

"He has someone else."

"He has a girlfriend?" Charlotte seethes.

"No!" I shake my head quickly.

"A kid?" Piper offers out.

I let out air I didn't realize I was holding.

"What then?"

I gulp. "You know Valeria Sánchez?"

"The movie star?" Charlotte asks.

11

"Yes."

"What about her?" Piper asks.

"She's his wife."

Piper's mouth hangs open. Charlotte's eyes go wide.

"Say something," I beg.

"His wife?" Piper shrieks.

"That piece of shit," Charlotte mutters.

"Shh. You promised you wouldn't go crazy. Remember, we are in a hospital."

Before I can say anything else, Charlotte and Piper spin and are leaving.

"Stop. You promised," I yell out.

"Oh, don't worry," Piper assures me. "We won't forget we are in a hospital, will we, Charlotte?"

"Nope," Charlotte calls.

Oh no. No, no, no!

"This isn't appropriate. Chase just got shot." I fall into step with them.

"Yep, we know," Charlotte says sweetly.

My gut is flipping.

We get to the lobby where Vivian's parents are talking to the doctors, and Noah, Xander, and Jamison are all in the conversation with them.

Jamison holds my gaze, and I close my eyes, trying to figure out how to warn him.

They are at the desk for a while. I sit between Charlotte and Piper and whisper, "You don't know the entire story."

"What's there to know?" Piper sneers.

"I got the only important fact, didn't you, Piper?" Charlotte replies and smiles at Xander as he winks at her from the desk.

"They are so dead," Piper mutters.

"Yep," Charlotte chirps.

"Seriously. You two aren't helping me right now."

Piper puts her arm around me. "Did you know he had a wife when he seduced you?"

"No, but..."

When he seduced me?

Before I can finish thinking, Charlotte leans in. "He's legally married to Valeria Sánchez. *The* Valeria Sánchez? Box-office extraordinaire? Swimsuit cover model? *That* Valeria Sánchez?

"Yes, her. But—"

"Time to go." Piper unwraps her arm and jumps up. The guys are all walking toward us, oblivious as to what is about to happen.

"Hospital," I whisper. "You promised."

Charlotte stands up as well. "Time to leave?"

Xander nods and puts his arms around her waist. "Yep. Time to get you home so you can rest."

"Hmm." She crosses her arms.

Xander seems confused. "What does that mean?"

"Oh, nothing."

Piper is giving Noah her death glare.

"Piper, what's going on?"

She focuses her glare on Jamison. "We all need to go outside."

"Outside?" Noah asks.

"Piper," I mumble and put my hand on my face.

"Yep. Outside the hospital," Charlotte agrees.

"Charlotte?" Xander asks.

"Out now. Everyone." Charlotte points.

"Let's at least use our manners and tell Vivian's parents bye," I say.

"We already did," Noah said.

"Come on." Piper grabs Charlotte's and my hands.

We give hugs and say our goodbyes, and Piper and Charlotte march right past the guys, shaking their heads and giving all three of them a death glare.

We're only ten feet outside the building when they spin and face Jamison.

"You're married?" Charlotte seethes.

"You're such a piece of shit," Piper snarls.

Jamison glances at me, hurt. I blink back tears.

"Don't you dare look at her like that!" Piper snaps.

"Piper—" Noah starts.

"Oh, no. You're not innocent in this."

Noah takes a deep breath.

"Nor you." Charlotte glares at Xander.

"How is this Noah's and my fault, Charlotte?"

"So neither of you knew about Mrs. Valeria Sánchez Lancott?" Charlotte arches an eyebrow at Xander.

Guilt passes over Noah and Xander's faces.

"Shh. Don't be throwing her name around and making it public knowledge," Jamison says.

Heat flares in Piper's face. "How dare you say that in front of Quinn."

"Do you even know the whole story, Piper?" Jamison demands.

"What? That you fucked our friend and didn't tell her you were married? That story?" Charlotte sneers.

Jamison looks to the sky.

"Quinn isn't someone's mistress," Piper yells.

"She isn't someone to use for sex, and that's it," Charlotte informs him.

Jamison's face reddens. "Yeah, I know Quinn isn't either of those."

"Quinn is someone you love, not someone you hide," Piper tells him.

"She's not just any girl. She's special," Charlotte cries out.

"Don't you think I know all this? I love her, for god's sake," Jamison protests.

"Oh, that's brilliant. You love her, and you're married." Piper glares.

"Piper!" Noah yells.

"Don't you dare, Noah!"

"You don't know—"

"What about your wife, Jamison? I'm sure you told Quinn lots of lies about how you love her and not your wife," Charlotte states.

"I've never loved my wife, and I do love Quinn, and if you knew the whole story, you would know that," Jamison replies.

"You're so full of shit," Charlotte yells.

"Charlotte, you don't know the truth," Xander says.

"The truth? The truth is he's married. Stop sticking up for him."

"Why are you even here? You should go home to your wife," Piper blasts Jamison.

"Stop! Everyone just stop!" I yell through my tears.

Jamison steps forward and pulls me close.

In a moment of weakness, I sink into his arms then realize what is happening. "Don't. Nothing has changed." I push him away as a river of tears flow down my face, and my heart breaks all over again.

Piper grabs my arm, and Charlotte grabs the other.

"The three of you can find another way home," Piper tells them and pulls me into her as she and Charlotte lead me to the car where Noah's driver is waiting.

2

Quinn

Eight Months Earlier

I'VE NEVER BEEN GOOD AT KEEPING MY EMOTIONS IN CHECK. I TRY to put on a good face and smile, but seeing Charlotte lying in a hospital bed, heavily medicated, with her foot in traction, on medication, add in my upset about Xander... I'm about to cry, and I don't want to in front of her. "I'm going to step out now. You get some rest, and I'll be back."

As soon as I get through the door, my tears fall down my cheeks. I'm almost to the elevator when he stops me.

"Quinn, wait up."

I wipe my face and turn.

"Are you okay?" Jamison asks.

I nod, but more tears fall.

He pulls me into his arms. "Everything will be okay. She's going to recover."

"I know," I sob.

"Shh." He strokes my hair.

I sink against his muscular pecs, and he tightens his arms around me. My heart beats faster from a mix of my emotions over Charlotte and the attraction I can't help but feel toward him.

One of my best friends is hurt, and I have wet panties. I'm seriously a horrible person.

I only met this man today, but the attraction started before I even met him.

Months ago, I had seen his picture and then saw him on Facetime in nothing but a Speedo when he was auctioned off for a charity date night. Piper was at the event in New York with Noah. Charlotte, Vivian, and I watched through the phone. Charlotte even bid on Xander.

Yep, I had admired him from afar. What wasn't to love? His chiseled face, green eyes, and dark wavy hair took my breath away. The muscles that bulged under his bronzed skin created one dirty scenario after another in my fantasies.

Jamison should be the new name for my B.O.B. Although I'm sure the motor is going to wear out soon since I haven't had any action in almost a year.

I assumed he would be a cocky asshole. Weren't all guys who had this much going on? Plus, he was friends with Noah, Xander, and Chase, who all had the cocky swagger. Granted, I only met Chase today, but I had assumed it from his picture, and being in his presence only confirms it.

Cocky guys aren't a turn-off. And it isn't that Noah, Xander, and Chase are assholes. They are good guys. But I expect their cockiness.

Jamison is throwing me for a loop. He's not cocky. If he is, I haven't seen it yet. He is quieter than the other guys. He thinks before he opens his mouth. And his eyes focus on me when I'm talking, and different expressions cross his face, which makes me think he's interested and paying attention to what I have to say.

There are so many things about Jamison I didn't expect.

The intense flutters that have been in my gut all day that aren't getting any lighter.

Or the way he gazes at me, causing me to think he might be attracted to me.

And the clean, woody scent of his skin should be bottled up and sold to the masses because it's been making my blood pump against my flesh.

It's like everything I've ever read in any of the steamy romance novels I edit is happening in real life, and I've never experienced it before. What I assumed is only a figment of authors' imaginations is smacking me in the face, and it's so inappropriate.

You're in the hospital getting your panties in a twist while your best friend is seriously injured. Something is wrong with you, Quinn.

"I'm getting your shirt wet," I say but don't move out of his grasp.

He strokes my hair some more. "It's just a shirt."

I pull back. "Sorry. I'm a mess."

"It's okay. You're allowed to be upset. It just shows what a good friend you are."

"Hospitals, weddings, and funerals I don't stand a chance at."

He chuckles. "I'll bring a box of tissues the next time we go to any of those events."

The next time? Adrenaline shoots through my veins.

Simmer down, Quinn. He's only joking.

I wipe under my eyes and try to compose myself.

"Why don't we step outside and get some air?" Jamison suggests.

"Sure. That sounds good." We walk past Noah and Chase, who are exchanging words. Jamison puts his hand on my back, sending a heat wave through my spine, and leads me past them.

"What is that all about?" I question him once we get outside.

"No idea. I'm sure we will find out."

I inhale deeply a few times, enjoying the fresh air.

"You look ready to do some yoga."

"Well, I do like my yoga."

His eyes drift over my body. "That doesn't surprise me."

Heat creeps into my face, and he licks his lip and points to a bench. "Let's go sit down."

I sit on the bench, and he sits next to me and stretches his arm across the back of the seat.

"Where are you staying while you're in town?"

"We haven't gotten that far yet. After Noah called this morning, I threw my stuff in a bag and rode in a cab to the private airport. I don't even know what I packed."

"I'm sure whatever you packed is fine to hang out around here."

I roll my eyes. "I'm sure you're right. No reason to worry about your wardrobe here."

He taps the wood near my shoulder. "Have you lived in Chicago long?"

"My entire life."

"Been to New York much?"

I shake my head. "Only Times Square once on New Year's Eve."

"Ouch!"

"Not a fan?"

"No paramedic or emergency responder is."

"I can understand that."

"You need to experience the city from a local's viewpoint."

My heart races.

"If you're going to be here awhile, I could show you all the good spots."

"You could?"

He smiles at me. "I could."

"Oh, crap!"

"What's wrong?"

"I just realized I never called into work." I pull out my phone and type an email to my boss.

Jamison doesn't say anything until I am done sending my email off. "What do you do?"

"I edit novels."

"What kind of novels."

"Romance novels."

He raises an eyebrow. "The hot ones or the clean ones?"

I cover my face with my hand and peek through my fingers. "Mostly the steamy ones."

His tongue that I'm dying to taste licks his lips again. "So, you practice yoga and edit sex scenes. Hmm."

"Hmm?"

He leans into me, his warm breath against my ear. "You might be one of the most interesting girls I've ever met." His face is right next to mine, and he doesn't move it.

If I just moved my mouth an inch, I wonder what would happen.

"Jamison," Chase calls, motioning us to come back into the hospital.

We turn, and once again, our mouths are inches from the other. Jamison scans my eyes. "To be continued."

I'm frozen, unable to move. I lick my lips, and he glances at my tongue. He stands then pulls me up, right into his chest.

He smells like sex on a stick. I'm pretty sure his pheromones are penetrating all my cells.

Releasing me, he steps away, and I immediately feel the chill from the lack of his body next to mine. But he quickly places his hand on my back and leads me inside.

Chase is waiting for us. "Noah went to get Vivian and Piper. Visiting hours are almost over. Our drivers should be here any minute."

"Where is Noah staying?"

"His penthouse fell through."

"Is that where Vivian and I are staying?"

"I was going to wait until Vivian was here—"

"Here for what?" Vivian comes around the corner.

Chase smiles at her. "Noah and I think it's best if you and Quinn stay at my place so you aren't involved in whatever is going on with their security issues."

Vivian and I both shake our heads.

"I have lots of room, and Jamison is staying at my place right now, too, during his remodel," Chase quickly adds.

Jamison, too? Hmm.

"Sorry. We didn't mean to be rude. That's very nice of you to have us," I tell him.

Vivian says, "Yes, thank you. Are you sure it isn't too much trouble?"

Chase gives her a cocky look. "Not at all."

Vivian's face flushes.

Noah and Piper appear.

"Your driver here yet?" Noah asks Chase.

He looks at his phone. "He already got the girls' bags from Lou. They are both waiting on the curb."

We all say goodbye, walk out to the cars that are waiting, and Vivian, Chase, Jamison, and I get into Chase's car.

It's turned dark. Vivian and I fall asleep, Vivian on Chase's lap and me on Jamison's. When we pull up to Chase's building, Jamison is stroking my hair. "Quinn, time to wake up."

I open my eyes to see the outline of his semi.

Oh shit. I spring up in the seat next to him, heat is scorching my face.

He softly laughs. "There isn't a fire."

"Where are Vivian and Chase?"

"They already went up. You were extra tired." His eyes are crinkling around the edges.

"Sorry." I open the door and step out on the curb.

"No sorry necessary." He stands next to me and takes my bag from Chase's driver.

"I can take that," I quickly say.

"No."

"No?"

"No."

So he's a gentleman, too?

"Thanks, Terry." He puts his hand on my lower back.

"Have a great night," the driver says as we walk away.

We get into the building, through security, and to the elevator. He punches in a code. No one is in it except us, but he stands right next to me and glances down.

"What?" I nervously ask.

"Hungry?"

To devour your body.

"I only had coffee today, so yes, I'm starving."

"Why didn't you say something? I would have gotten you some food."

"That's sweet of you, but I don't think I could have eaten at the hospital. Too many nerves."

"You want to go out or stay in?"

Out as in a date? No, he's being a good host. Get your mind out of the gutter, Quinn.

The elevator opens. "I'm up for anything."

I don't know what to make of his amused grin. We step out into the small corridor, and he opens the door into the penthouse.

"Wow. This is beautiful." The windows overlook Manhattan, and the night sky is twinkling with the lights of the city. Just like Chase said, there is plenty of room. The place is huge.

Jamison guides me into the kitchen where Vivian is sitting on a barstool, and Chase is pouring her a glass of red wine.

"Want a drink?" he asks me.

"That would be great. I'll have a glass of whatever that is."

"It's a Malbec."

"That works."

"Jamison?"

"Sounds good."

Jamison pulls a barstool out for me to sit down then walks over to the fridge and peers inside. Shutting the refrigerator, he turns toward us. "Ladies, you want to go out for dinner, or do you want my famous apple-grilled cheese sandwiches?"

"They are pretty amazing," Chase tells us.

"By all means, show us your skills, then," Vivian says.

I take a sip of wine. A delicious mix of blackberry, plum, and cherry hits my tongue, followed by a smoky finish. I moan.

"Jesus, Quinn. Don't have an orgasm over the wine," Vivian teases me.

"What? It's delicious."

"We can tell that."

Jamison's eyes are full of heat. He gulps.

To deflect, I stand up and walk around the island and join Jamison. "What can I do to help?"

He blinks. "You don't have to help. Just relax."

"What if I want to know the secret to these famous sandwiches?"

He pulls a drawer open and withdraws two aprons. He sets one on the counter, turns me so my back is to him, and slips the other one over my head then secures the ties. He leans forward so his face is right next to mine. "I hope you like to chop?"

"Sure. I can chop."

He puts the other apron on.

"That's our cue." Chase grabs Vivian's hand.

"Where are we going?"

"Away from the kitchen so they can slave over our dinner."

They leave the room.

Jamison sets a few red apples in front of me along with a cutting board and knife. "We need thin slices."

"Got it." I wash the apples, dry them, then get to work while Jamison butters bread and puts it in a skillet.

Suddenly, his hands slide from my biceps down to my wrists then over my hands. My nostrils flare with his clean woody scent, and my pulse beats in my neck.

What is he doing?

"You're going to chop your fingers off."

"Is that right?" I respond quietly.

His head crosses over my shoulder, and his cheek is right next to mine. Jamison's so close to me, the hardness of his manhood is digging into my back. "Let me show you." His nimble fingers glide over mine. One set of hands grips the apple and the other clasps the knife.

Breathe, Quinn.

When the entire apple is ready, he sets the knife down and holds a slice to my lips. I take a bite then he pops the rest into his mouth.

I chew, swallow then, without thinking, I spin into him. His hands move down and plant on the counter, on both sides of my waist. I tilt my head up.

My heart is beating so hard I'm sure he can hear it.

"You're all set to be a sous chef now."

I slowly nod.

The fire alarm starts going off and he spins away from me. A black cloud of smoke pours out of the pan. He turns the gas off and dumps the contents of the skillet in the sink then turns on the overhead exhaust.

Vivian and Chase come running in.

"What's going on?" Chase asks.

"I burned the bread. No biggie," Jamison casually says.

"That's a lot of smoke," Vivian comments and gives me a knowing look, but I ignore her and pick up the second apple.

Where there's smoke, there's fire, runs through my head, but I'm not sure why.

3

Jamison

MY DICK IS IN A STATE OF CHAOS. FROM THE MOMENT I LAY EYES on Quinn, I tell it to stay down, but it isn't listening.

Quinn isn't just gorgeous with her wavy strawberry blonde hair, blue doe eyes, and pouty lips. She's a mix of fiery but sweet. Innocent yet sophisticated. Kind but sassy.

Xander is in a coma with a brain injury, and all I can think about is how I want to get this girl alone and find out everything about her.

And when I do get her alone, she tells me that she does yoga and edits sex scenes for a living.

I could have guessed the yoga, but...*exactly how flexible is she?*

Throughout the day, a sexy blush fills her face whenever I catch her looking or if I get too close. She seems inexperienced, but she reads and makes suggestions about how to make sex scenes hotter.

Jesus. How many fantasies does she have that I can help her play out?

On the way home, her face lies on my dick. I should have earned a medal for the amount of constraint it took for me not to unzip my pants and have her lick me like a lollipop before deep throating me when I woke her up.

And then she moans.

She sits in Chase's kitchen and fucking moans with her eyes shut.

I think my cock is about to burst out of my pants.

After that, I can't help myself and have to not only touch her but press against her, the moment we are alone.

I'm about to kiss her when the fire alarm goes off. And then Chase and Vivian run in, so the moment is over.

Quinn and I finish cooking dinner without anything else burning. The four of us eat and have another glass of wine. It's getting late, and Chase says he will show Vivian to her room.

I stand up and lift Quinn's bag.

"Take it, that's my hint it's bedtime?"

"I'm not tired. Are you tired after the nap you had?"

Please say you aren't tired.

She hesitates but then says, "No."

I take her hand, pull her down the hall, and drop her bag on her bed. "Put on your jammies and come down to my place."

"Your place?"

"Yes. I'm in a separate wing."

"A separate wing?" she cries out.

"Yes."

When she's done gaping, she says, "Okay. Give me a minute."

I step out of her room and shut the door.

"Great!" I hear her mutter before she opens the door and lets out a big sigh. "I didn't pack any pajamas."

"You did say you weren't sure what you packed."

"I knew I forgot something."

I clasp her hand. "No worries. You can wear one of my T-shirts."

"Oh. Okay. Thanks."

We move through two hallways to my living quarters.

"Holy…"

"What?"

"This is the size of my apartment."

I laugh.

"Sorry."

"It's okay."

"So, you live here?"

"Just while my place is under construction."

"Is that a palace, too?"

I smile at her but don't say anything.

"Oh. Sorry. My mouth sometimes doesn't work right." Her face flushes.

I'm sure your mouth works just fine.

She's adorable when she's flustered.

The red in her cheeks deepens.

She looks away and takes a deep breath.

I don't want her to be anxious. I tug her into my bedroom. "Let's get you that T-shirt."

"Um...all right."

In my walk-in closet, I open a drawer. "Take your pick."

She reaches in and finds a stack of T-shirts. Running her fingers over them, she finally pulls one from the middle. "This one."

"Why that one?"

"It's the softest."

"Okay. Get changed." I leave her in the closet and head for the kitchen where I grab two bottles of water out of the fridge. Then I throw an indie music channel on my speakers.

Quinn emerges wearing my New York First Responders Charity Auction T-shirt hanging off one of her shoulders. Her creamy skin is on display, and I have to hold myself back from grabbing her and licking her shoulder. The T-shirt hits mid-thigh and I scan her bare legs and feet. She catches me ogling her and her blush creeps back in her face.

"You're pretty cute when you blush."

She bites her lip, and my pants tighten.

"Are you getting in your pajamas, or am I the only one?"

"Sure. I sleep naked." I take my shirt off and unbuckle my pants, and her mouth drops open. Her head bounces from my bare chest to the wall, to my chest again. I try to stifle laughter.

"What is so funny."

"You look like you're going to have a heart attack. I'm just teasing you. Not about sleeping naked, but I'll go put some clothes on." I wink and hand her a bottle of water as I pass her. "If you want something else besides water, let me know or help yourself."

"Water is good. Thanks."

I throw on a pair of shorts and a T-shirt.

When I come out, Quinn is standing in front of the window, nervously tapping her fingers against her thigh.

I walk up behind her and put my hand on top of hers so it's flat against her thigh. I wrap my other arm around her waist, and she inhales sharply.

She fits so perfectly against me.

I lean into her ear. "I won't bite. Promise. Unless you want me to."

She releases her breath and turns into me.

I could kiss her.

I want to kiss her.

I need to kiss her.

But her eyes flick left and right, so instead, I stroke her cheek. "Let's go talk."

"Talk?" She reddens again.

I chuckle. "Yeah. I speak. You speak. We talk."

"Funny."

I guide her over to the couch then open up the ottoman and pull out an oversized fuzzy blanket. I slide the ottoman up against the sofa so she has to put her legs on it then I sit on the couch next to her, throw the blanket on us, and put my arm around her.

"Didn't expect you to have a big, fuzzy blanket. Is it yours or Chase's?"

"Mine."

"Impressive." She grins at me.

"Quinn, Quinn, Quinn..." I put my legs on the ottoman.

"Jamison, Jamison, Jamison..." she mocks me and places her legs on top of mine.

"What's your story?" I ask.

"My story?"

"Yeah. Your story. Not the stories you edit, although you can tell me about those later." I wiggle my brows.

"Ha, ha!"

"Tell me all about you."

She shrugs. "What do you want to know?"

"Everything."

Quinn finally says, "Can you be more specific?"

Let's start with the most important question.

"Boyfriend?"

"Would I be sitting half-naked with you if I had one?"

"Are you trying to give me a visual?"

She laughs.

"Okay. No boyfriend. You're recently broken up, I take it?"

"Ummm...no. Why do you think that?"

She must be like Chase, then.

"Are you the no-relationship girl?"

She furrows her brows. "No. Why would you ask that?"

"A girl like you shouldn't be single for long."

She rolls her eyes.

"What was that face for?"

"I've not had a serious boyfriend for over a year, and I'm almost approaching a year without sex. It wasn't even good. I think the motor on my vibrator is going to die out. I'm definitely not a hot commodity right now." She slaps her hand over her mouth and turns purple. Her eyes close and she looks toward the window.

What the... No way. How the hell does a girl like this not have sex for almost a year? And no boyfriend? And jeez, if the motor on her vibrator is going to wear out then...oh fuck. My desire to make her orgasm all night long just grew tenfold.

"There must be a bunch of douchebags in Chicago, then."

She slowly looks at me. "Why do you say that?"

I lean in closer. "Have you consulted the mirror lately? Besides your killer body, beautiful face, and charming personality, you also are a really great friend, which means you probably are a perfect girlfriend. So yeah, Chicago must be full of douchebags."

Come on. Lean an inch in, and I'll do the rest.

It's so quiet, the tick of the clock echoes in the room.

She doesn't move. *How long has it been since she's been kissed? Properly kissed?*

"I want to kiss you."

Her breath hitches.

"Can I kiss you?"

"Yes."

I weave my hands into her hair and tilt my head to the side before pressing my lips gently into hers several times.

"Breathe," I remind her, and she exhales.

Jesus, this girl is so fucking perfect.

I part her lips open and slide my tongue against hers.

She runs her hands through my hair, lightly pulling it, and circles my mouth with her tongue, pushing deeper into me like I'm a Tootsie Pop, and she needs to get to the center.

My adrenaline spikes. My cock hardens.

She turns, bends her knee up on the couch, and rotates her body on me.

"You're the best kisser on earth," I tell her.

"Yeah?"

"Hands down." And she is. I pull her so she's straddling me and the smooth skin of her thighs slides on both sides of mine. I move my hands under the T-shirt and against her naked back, pushing her closer to me.

She moans in my mouth, and my cock pulses against her panties.

This girl is going to wreck me. She has to be the sexiest creature alive.

Her sex is already damp. I can feel her heat penetrating through my shorts. She grinds against my cock, breathing harder, whimpering in my mouth.

I groan. *God damn. I need to make this girl orgasm before she dry humps me and makes me blow my wad.*

Reaching into her panties to palm her perfect, round ass, I move my other hand to the front of her body. I trace her slit, over the thin material soaked with her juices, then press her clit. She shudders and lets out another moan.

I don't think I need to ask. I'm pretty sure what her answer will be. She needs it. Fuck, she deserves it. But I check anyway. "I want to make you come all night. Can I?"

"Oh God," she breathes, pulsing against my finger.

"Is that a yes?" I ask between kisses.

"Yes," escapes her lips.

Without wasting any time, I slide past the silky material and into her slippery folds.

She clenches instantly.

"Relax, doll," I tell her.

She takes a shaky breath and releases her hold on my finger.

"That's it," I praise.

I would slip another one in her, but she's tight, which only makes my cock harder. I circle my thumb on her nub, and she rocks her hips, trembling and moaning.

I pull my hand away from her ass and move it to her head.

"You're so sexy," I murmur, and she responds by kissing me deeper.

I move my thumb faster and curl my finger inside her.

"Yes...oh...yes..." she squeaks, blinking rapidly.

I could slow her down, but I plan on giving her so many orgasms, she can't walk in the morning. So I swipe faster and harder.

It isn't long before she convulses in my arms. Her mouth forms a gorgeous O. Her eyes roll back in her head as she screams out my name.

She collapses against me, burying her face in the crook of my neck.

"You're beautiful. I'm going to take care of you all night." I hold her tight to me, not wanting to let her go.

4

Quinn

I'M PANTING INTO HIS NECK, AND MY HEART IS THUMPING HARD. *I can't believe I came that fast.*

"You're beautiful. I'm going to take care of you all night." Jamison kisses my head, holding me tightly.

All night. I've never had a one-night stand. I can hear my mother's voice in my head saying, "Don't be easy, or you'll never be anything more to a man than sex."

But it's not like I even live in the same city as this guy, so maybe this is the perfect time for it to be just sex.

Jamison is stroking my hair, and I slowly pull out of his neck. He kisses me then pushes his forehead to mine. "I want to take you to my bed. Can I do that?"

I don't answer, and he quickly says, "You don't have to do anything you don't want to."

Somehow, I find a bit of courage in me. "What do you want to do to me in your bed?"

"Everything. But only if you want it." He pauses and then says, "Do you want it?"

"Yes," my hoarse voice fills the air.

His lips turn upward. He kisses me then kicks the ottoman out of the way. In a swift move, he stands up with me in his arms and continues to kiss me while carrying me to his bedroom.

Within seconds, he removes my T-shirt and bra then takes off his shirt, revealing his torso full of muscle and well-defined pecs and arms. I swallow hard. Months of trying to remember what he looked like on stage through a FaceTime video didn't prepare me for his in-person perfection.

Like a magnet, I reach out for him, fondling his warm skin, trailing my fingers over his ab muscles.

He traces my areola as my nipple hardens and puckers.

"I guess it's my lucky night that there are only douchebags in Chicago."

"I never asked you if you have a girlfriend."

"No girlfriend. No one special."

I cup his face. I don't know why I tell him this, but I say, "I've never done this before with someone I just met."

"We can stop at any time. You can stay in my bed all night, and we don't have to do anything if you don't want to."

"No. I'm okay."

"All right. You tell me at any point to stop, and don't feel bad about it. I don't want you to regret anything tomorrow."

I pull him close, loving the way my bare skin merges into his warm flesh. Our lips fit together so easily, it's like they were created to do so. The flutters I've felt all day around him are the strongest they've been, as his kisses light up my every cell.

Desire surges through me. No one has ever kissed me like Jamison. It's as if his lips are worshiping me, staking a claim on me, and ruining me all at the same time.

Any man I kiss from this point forward, I will compare to him. There's no way they can even compete.

"I could kiss you all night," he murmurs against my lips.

"I could kiss you all night," I repeat.

"I love your lips, but I want to kiss you everywhere." He brushes my hair back. I shudder slightly as his lips move across my jaw to my earlobe. "Any man who's let you slip by is a fool," he murmurs in my ear before moving lower onto my neck.

Fireworks burst in all my nerves as his lips brush my collarbone and down to my breasts, licking and sucking me so expertly, I quickly moan. I grasp his hair and kiss his head. My breath rises and falls rapidly.

He moves lower, kissing my stomach then licking my belly button.

Thank God I got a wax a few days ago.

He inhales then groans, kisses my slit, slides his hands under my thighs, and wraps them around my hips.

I'm soaked, throbbing, and heat is rushing through me. I push my knees farther out, opening up for him, desperate for what he's about to give me.

His tongue lashes me, gliding throughout my folds, dipping into my hole, flicking my clit.

I'm whimpering, gripping his hair, and bucking into his face. My mouth is a permanent O, as sounds I've never heard myself make come flying out of it.

Tingles move through me, sizzling, crackling, ready to burst into pools of pleasure.

His lips latch onto my clit while his tongue continues to flick me.

"Oh...oh...don't stop...please don't stop," I cry out.

I grip his hair tighter. My back arches off the bed as I grind into his mouth.

Jamison holds me tight as adrenaline rushes through my veins, sending me soaring over the edge.

I'm shaking and trying to catch my breath when he shimmies up my naked torso. His green eyes bore into mine before he grabs my head and quickly sticks his tongue full of my orgasm in my mouth.

"You're perfect and sexy as hell," he proclaims between kisses.

I'm still breathing hard, and I reach down to his shorts, sticking my hand inside and stroking his hard cock. I rub the tip and feel his precum. Then slide my hand farther, surprised at how large he feels.

Is he going to fit in me? Maybe because I haven't had sex in so long he feels so big?

I stroke him some more and push on the vein I can feel from his base to his tip, and a deep, throaty groan emerges.

"I want you, Quinn. Can I have you?"

"Yes. I want you, too," I breathlessly tell him.

Is this really happening?

He bucks his hips up to push his shorts down and leans his naked body against me. Continuing to kiss me, he reaches over to his nightstand, opens the drawer, and fumbles around to find the condom. Bringing it to his teeth, he tears the package open, rolls the condom over his cock.

The tip of him pushes against my hole. "Wait," I whisper.

He stops and scans my eyes. "We can stop."

I shake my head. "No. Just..."

He caresses my cheek with the back of his hand. "Quinn, we can stop."

I shake my head harder and blurt out, "I don't think I've been with anyone as big as you. Can you go slow...going in?"

He tries to bite back a smile.

My face burns with embarrassment.

He leans into my ear and quietly says, "I was already planning on it."

I let out a breath. "Okay."

"Wrap your legs around me, doll."

He scoops me up and pulls me tight to him.

"Relax and tell me if it doesn't feel good." He sinks into me, inch by inch, pushing in and pulling back a bit, letting my body sheathe around him.

"Oh God," I moan, palming his back.

"Fuck, you're tight," he growls.

He isn't even all the way in, and I'm pulsing against him. I slide my hand down his warm skin, rock my hips up, and guide him deeper into me.

He groans, and I gasp. My lip shakes, and he takes it between his teeth, gently biting it.

"I lied. I'm going to bite you."

He closes his eyes and thrusts his hips a few times, driving deeper and deeper into me.

I tighten my arms around him as his length and girth fill me so much I get slightly dizzy.

Pushing his forehead to mine, he murmurs, "You're amazing."

I can't reply. I'm blinking my eyes trying to refocus, my mouth is once again in an O, and I can't stop whimpering in his arms. I've never felt the rushes of pleasure I'm feeling as he thrusts into me, increasing his speed, pounding me harder.

Is that my...? Oh God, yes, that has to be my G-spot.

"Jamison," I cry out, shaking under him as he tightens his arms around me.

"Oh, you're so good."

"Jamison," I say again, oscillating over and over as endorphins are crashing through my system.

"That's it, doll." He thrusts harder, and I spin further into Wonderland, gripping my limbs around him tighter.

I orgasm so many times, I don't know where one ends and the other one begins as he continues to fill me, sliding against all my spasming nerves, reaching my sweet spot that I never knew existed before now.

Our skin glistens with a sheen of sweat as the heat of our flesh melt against each other.

He pushes his forehead to mine, and his warm breath pants hard against mine. With a final thrust, he erupts, swelling against my walls and forcing me into one last climax.

We lie against each other, trying to find air, our chests heaving, staring at each other. I'm still quivering.

How is it possible to feel that good?

Jamison kisses me, pulls out of me, and rolls over. He removes the condom and gets up and throws it in the trash. Pulling the covers back, he motions with his hand. "Scoot under."

I scoot under, and he climbs next to me then pulls me into his arms. "Tell me everything about you."

I turn so I can see him.

"Tell me what you want to know, and I'll tell you."

"Everything, Quinn. I want to know everything about you, and don't leave out any details."

5

Jamison

I'M CONVINCED THAT ALL THE MEN IN CHICAGO ARE COMPLETE idiots for not snagging this girl. Jeez. Can she get any sexier? Any sweeter? Any sassier? This girl has got it all going on. To top it off, she orgasmed so many times on my cock, I lost track of how many times she came.

I tell her I want to know everything about her, and I mean it.

"What's your family like?"

"I don't remember my father. My mom raised my brother and me on her own. She was strict with me, but my brother was worse than her in some ways."

Her father left them? What a piece of shit.

I tighten my arm around her and stroke her hip. "What do you mean?"

"My mom had my brother. He's four years older than me. Then she had me. My father left her when I was only six months old. He..." She looks away and inhales.

My heart thumps in my chest, waiting for her to speak.

Quinn turns back but doesn't meet my gaze. Pain laces her face and her voice. "He had another family. My mom was his mistress and didn't even know it."

Whoa. What an asshole.

I pull her closer to me. "I'm sorry. That's a horrible thing for you to go through."

"My brother had it worse, I think. He remembers him. At least I don't have those demons in my head."

I kiss her cheek. "So, your mom and brother were strict with you?"

"I had to be in the house at nine o'clock. If I was a minute late, I was grounded. I wasn't allowed to date until I was eighteen. My cousin had to take me to my proms. It was so embarrassing."

I chuckle. "No. Not your cousin!"

She elbows me. "It's not funny."

"I'm sorry, but you have to admit, it is a little."

"The worst part is my cousin is really good-looking, and he hooked up at both my proms with my friends. And my brother insisted on volunteering to chaperone. The guy I liked asked me to dance, and after the first song was over, my brother came over and cut in."

"What? Stop it. You're making this up." I slap my hand over my mouth not to laugh, but tears of laughter fill my eyes.

Quinn slaps my arm. "It's not funny. I'm scarred for life."

"I bet you are," I agree with her as a tear rolls down my cheek.

"I'm glad you can find my life so amusing," she sarcastically says.

I wipe my face. "I'm sorry. So your mom and brother didn't let you have a life. But you didn't go crazy and rebel once you moved out?"

"You mean, did I start having orgies and become a drug addict while listening to rock and roll?"

Oh, sweet girl, I know you did nothing of that sort.

"I had a partial scholarship. My mom had a good job but not enough money for college, so I had to pay for school myself. My brother tried to help as much as he could, but he was just getting started in his career. Between school and my side jobs, I didn't have time for much else."

"What were your side jobs?"

She covers her hands in her face. "Ugh. I don't want to tell you."

"Why? Did you become a stripper or something?" I tease. *No way this girl did anything of the sort. Not that I would judge her if she had.*

"Ha, ha. Funny."

I lean into her ear. "You can put your stripper fantasies to work anytime for me."

She elbows me in the rib cage.

"Ouch!"

"Sorry but not sorry."

"Okay. So, what were these jobs? Don't deviate."

She groans and puts her face in her hands again.

"Come on. You can tell me."

"I worked at a fast-food place."

"Okay. What's wrong with that?"

"It was a chicken place."

"And?"

"They made me be the chicken who stands on the side of the road, waving down traffic."

"No! You didn't!" My cheeks are starting to hurt from laughing so hard.

"It was horrible."

"I bet." I wipe the moisture off my face.

"What was your other job?"

"I was also a librarian for the college."

"So you always loved books? That's how you became an editor?"

"Yes and no."

I raise an eyebrow.

"I've always loved books. It wasn't my dream to be an editor. I just kind of fell into it. It was the next best thing."

"What did you dream of being?"

"It's unrealistic. You'll laugh."

I lift her chin. "I won't. I promise."

She hesitates.

"Tell me."

"I wanted to be a fiction writer. I even wrote a bunch of books."

"You haven't published them?"

"No. I tried when I was in college and got turned down by all the traditional publishing companies. I don't have the connections."

"Why don't you self-publish?"

"Be an indie author?"

"Yeah. Those are the only books I read now."

Her eyes widen. "You read books?"

I chuckle. "Do you think I can't read?"

"I don't think I know any men who read books."

"You're not making me think any higher of these guys in Chicago."

"You seriously read indie authors?"

"All the time. I love finding a good undiscovered author. It's like rooting for the underdog."

"Hmm."

"You should do it."

She doesn't respond to that. "What kind of books do you read?"

"Thrillers mostly. Some Urban Fantasy. *Fifty Shades* was pretty good though."

"You read *Fifty Shades*?" she cries out.

"Yep. But I read it before it got famous."

She gapes.

She's so cute when she gets surprised.

"You know she self-published it first, right?

"Yes, but..."

"But what?"

"That's a one-off thing. Most people who self-publish never even sell two hundred and fifty copies of their book."

"That may be true, but I know plenty of indie authors who have huge cult-like followings."

"Really?"

"You should publish your books."

She gapes.

"You should."

She doesn't say anything.

"So, do you like editing?"

"It's okay. The company I work for is eh. But it's not exactly a thriving job market for editors who need benefit packages. Anyway, enough about me. What is your family like?"

"My mom and dad have been married forever and are getting close to retirement. I have four sisters."

"Four?"

I nod. "Yep. They are all older and liked to emasculate me as a child."

"Emasculate you?"

"Yep. I had to play dress-up, dolls, everything except what I wanted to. I can dress and undress a Barbie doll in record time."

"I bet you were a total perv with those poor Barbies."

I wink. "Perks of the job. So, what's your favorite color?"

"Pink."

"Favorite meal?"

"A greasy burger and steak fries with a milkshake."

She eats that and keeps her perfect body?

"Really? You just became the coolest girl ever."

"What's yours?"

"I'll take a greasy burger any day. What's your favorite ice cream?"

"Cake batter," she says.

"Hold on a minute."

I run out to the kitchen for a pint out of the freezer and a spoon. Then I bring it back into the bedroom. "You have to try this. My friend owns this company, and it's the best." I sit with my legs crossed on the bed and feed her a spoonful of the ice cream.

She closes her eyes, licks her lips, and moans.

I need to record that sound so I can listen to it when she's gone.

"I'm going to call you when you go back to Chicago."

"You are?"

"Yeah, just so I can listen to you moan. You should give me your phone number right now."

A blush crosses her face.

She has no clue how sexy she is.

I take a bite of ice cream and scoop another one for her and feed her again. Leaning forward, I pull her down flat on the bed.

She giggles. "What are you doing?"

I take a spoon of ice cream and spread it across her breast. Her nipple hardens, and I trace the spoon around it.

She inhales and bites down on her lip.

Dipping down, I slowly lick it off her, gliding my tongue on the fullness of her breast before focusing on her areola and finally enclosing my lips on her tit.

Her gorgeous chest rises and falls faster while she strokes my shoulder with her warm hand.

"I didn't think this ice cream could taste any better, but it just did," I tell her and bring my lips to her.

For a girl who has limited experience, at least I'm assuming she does from what she's told me tonight, she kisses like a porn star. She knows exactly what to do with her tongue, lips, and even her teeth at times, and I've never experienced kisses so hot. It's as if I'm her only possession in life, and she's claiming me as her own.

My semi is back. "How does a girl who took her cousin to prom kiss like that?"

She pushes me off her and grabs the ice cream out of my hand. She dips her fingers in the pint, pulls out a chunk, and smears it from my neck, over my torso, and onto my cock and balls.

"You're going to have to lick that off now."

A mischievous grin forms on her face and she bends down and flicks her tongue all over my balls, shaft, and cap before deep throating me a few times.

"Fuuuuuck," I groan.

She trails her tongue up my body. By the time she gets to my neck, I'm convinced she's the sexiest woman on earth, and precum is slipping out of my dick.

I pull her mouth to mine, urgently kissing her, cupping her butt and moving my hands down her thighs before positioning them on either side of my hips.

I grab a condom out of the nightstand while still kissing her, and she grabs it from me and rips it open with her teeth.

Where did this girl come from?

She slides it over my rod, and I groan.

"You're pretty dirty from your ice cream," she murmurs against my lips.

"Yeah?" I breathe.

"Mm-hmm." She rolls her tongue around my mouth a few times, and all my nerves wake back up.

"What are you going to do about that?"

She leans into my ear. "I'm going to ride you dirty."

6

Quinn

VISITING HOURS AREN'T UNTIL NOON, AND NEITHER JAMISON NOR I set the alarm. We spent most of the night having sex and talking. It's after five in the morning by the time we fall asleep.

"Jamison," Chase bellows.

I sit up in bed, startled, pulling the covers over my breasts and not sure what else to do. *Oh no. This is not happening.*

"Jamison, you—" Chase stops in the doorway to the bedroom.

Heat rises in my face.

Chase beams. "Good morning, Quinn."

I want to die right now.

Jamison slowly wakes up. He moves his hand under the covers and rubs my thigh. "Ever heard of knocking?"

Chase chuckles. "Sorry, didn't think you had company."

Heat singes my cheeks. I glance between Jamison and Chase and slide under the covers so my head is hidden.

Jamison continues to rub my thigh. "You have five seconds to tell me why you're here."

"We're leaving in an hour for the hospital. Unless you want to go separately?"

"I'll shoot you a text in a few minutes."

"All right."

"Wait."

Silence ensues. Jamison's fingers creep closer to my sex, and I'm cursing myself because my lower body pulses, but I want to hit his hand away as well. I'm sure Chase can't see it, but still.

This is so embarrassing.

"This isn't anyone's business unless Quinn decides it is," Jamison says.

"Noted. Mum's the word. I'll watch for your text."

I stay under the covers as the main door to the apartment clicks shut.

Jamison puts his head under the sheet, kissing my thigh, stomach, breast, and finally, giving me a peck on the mouth. "Don't freak out."

"I'm going to die of embarrassment now."

"I'm not embarrassed."

"Yeah. You're a guy."

"I don't think that should matter."

"Our friends are in the hospital, and we just met."

"I'm sorry. I didn't want you to have any regrets from last night."

"I don't," I quickly say.

"No?"

I cup his face in my hands. "No."

"Good. I like you."

"I like you, too."

"No, I mean really like you."

"You do?"

"Mm-hmm."

"Feeling is mutual."

He kisses me again, this time with heat and passion. Between kisses, he murmurs, "What should I tell Chase? Are we going with them or separate?"

I wrap my arms around him. "We probably should go with them."

"Says who?" He moves his hand right near my already dripping sex.

"We might stay in bed all day if we don't go with them."

"That would make us bad friends, huh?" He slips his tongue around my mouth.

"Mm-hmm. I have to shower."

"Me, too. How much time do you need after your shower, to be ready?"

His dexterous fingers shimmy across my slit. I gasp as he sticks two fingers in me. "T-twenty minutes?"

"Perfect. Let's go shower, and I'll make sure you have twenty minutes."

"Okay," I breathlessly tell him.

My clit is already sensitive, and he circles his thumb on it.

"Oh..." I widen my legs, bucking into his hand.

Within thirty seconds, he has me convulsing in his arms.

When I stop shaking, he throws the covers off us, grabs a condom from the nightstand, shoots a text message off then stands up with a full-on erection.

He reaches for my hand. "Let's go, doll. I want to maximize my shower time with you."

———

Jamison sneaks down to my room for my suitcase. I get ready in his place. I'm putting on my eyeliner when he comes into the bathroom.

Leaning down, he kisses my forehead. "I'm going to make a smoothie for the road. Do you want one?"

"Sure."

"Okay. I'll meet you out in the kitchen." He kisses my lips. "You are beautiful, by the way."

"With eyeliner on only one eye?"

He grins. "Yep. See you out there."

I continue to get ready, thinking about everything that has happened in the last twenty-four hours.

While I have zero experience with one-night stands, I have a feeling that this isn't typical. I can't help but wonder if this could lead somewhere.

But I live in Chicago, and he lives in New York.

Ugh.

Jamison has every quality I've ever wanted in a man. My infatuation with him before meeting him was all lust-driven, but now that I've gotten to know him, it's different.

He's kind, sweet, pays attention to me, and seems to always put me first. And unless he's putting on a show, he appears to really like me.

It's just my luck that we're several states apart, and he's the only man I've ever had mind-blowing sex with.

I finish getting ready and debate about what to do with my suitcase. I decide to leave it in his room in case Vivian is in the hallway. I don't want her or anyone else to know what happened.

As much as I want to shut my mother's voice in my head up, all I keep hearing is, "Don't be easy, or you'll never be anything more to a man than sex."

It figures that the one man I choose to be easy with is the one man I want to be something more to.

Lost in thought, I turn the corner and run smack into Vivian.

"There you are." She glances around. "Did you two have a fun time?"

I try to play dumb. "What are you talking about?"

She giggles. "Your suitcase isn't in your room and your bed is perfectly made. There was no sign of you anywhere in that room. There's only one place you could have been. Spill it."

I put my hands over my face. "Please don't say anything to anyone."

"I won't, but why do you look so embarrassed?"

"I just met him," I whisper.

"Quinn. It isn't 1950." She sneezes, pulls a tissue out of her pocket, and blows her nose.

"I know."

She elbows me. "So. I need details!"

I avoid answering her. "What about you and Chase?"

She smirks at me. "I slept in my room like a good girl."

"Vivian," I groan.

"I'm just teasing you. Seriously, you need to chill out, Quinn."

"Please don't tell anyone," I ask her again.

She puts her hand on my shoulder. "Okay. I won't."

"Thanks. It was bad enough Chase walked in on us."

"What?"

"Yeah, while I was naked in bed."

She covers her mouth and stifles a giggle.

"He didn't tell you?"

"No."

I sigh. "That makes me feel better, then. Hopefully, he keeps his mouth shut."

"No one would think badly of you, Quinn."

"Can we drop this?"

"Sure. Are you ready to go?"

"Yes."

We walk down the hall and into the kitchen. Jamison hands me a smoothie. I avoid Chase's gaze.

"Quinn, you all set to go, or do you need a jacket?" Chase asks.

"I'm good." Heat creeps into my face again.

"You should probably get a coat. It's cold out," Jamison tells me.

"All right. It's hanging on the coatrack by the front door. I'll grab it on the way out."

"Do you need your purse or your phone?" Chase asks.

"Both." I avoid his gaze again.

"Quinn, are you going to avoid looking at Chase all day? He didn't intentionally walk in on you," Vivian protests.

Jamison raises his eyebrow to me.

"Thanks, Vivian. Way to keep my business on the down-low."

"Sorry, but it's not polite, and we are staying at his house. Besides, if you do that at the hospital, Piper is going to be all up in your business."

I sigh and turn to Chase. "I'm sorry."

He nods. "It's okay. I'm not going to say anything to anyone. I promise."

"Okay. Thanks."

"In fact, why don't the four of us make a pact that whatever happens in this house stays in this house. We can all relax, then," Chase says.

"I'm good with that."

"Me, too," Vivian says.

"Agree." Jamison winks at me.

Chase grins at us. "Well, now that we got that out of the way, lets go spend an exciting day at the hospital."

CHARLOTTE IS ON A LOT OF PAIN MEDICATIONS AND MOVES IN AND out of sleep all day. Anytime she wakes up, she asks about Xander and cries when we tell her nothing has changed.

Xander is still in a coma.

Visiting hours last until 4 p.m. Noah and Piper were invited to Noah's New York assistant Nixon's house for dinner. They have a new baby, and he said it was easier for them to come over than go out.

We part ways and are soon back in Chase's car.

"I think it's time to hit the town and show these ladies the real New York," Jamison says.

Vivian sneezes. Chase hands her a wad of tissues from his pocket.

She laughs. "Stocking up?"

"I think you're coming down with a cold. You've been sneezing all day. Your throat hurt?"

She wipes her red nose. Her eyes are watering.

He puts a hand on her forehead then lays the back of his hand on her cheek. "You're warm."

"I'm okay."

He turns in his seat and pulls her back on him. "Just rest. You guys go out. We're staying in."

"We can go." Vivian sneezes again. "Or, you can go without me."

"Shh. Don't be silly. I can go out anytime."

Jamison looks at me. "Want to go out and see the town?"

"Sure. That sounds fun."

He winks, and butterflies go crazy in my stomach.

I'm sad Vivian is sick, but a part of me is excited to go out with Jamison alone.

When we get back home, Jamison and I head over to his apartment. As soon as we get through the door, he spins me into him, his lips crushing into mine.

I wrap my arms around him, and he pulls me tighter to him. His growing erection is poking my stomach.

"I've been dying to do that all day," he murmurs and teases my tongue some more.

I moan as his cock pulses against me.

His hands slip down and cup my ass. "I'm glad I get to take you on a real date."

Yes! It is a date!

"A date, huh?"

"Yep."

I giggle. "Will there be perks?"

He groans. "If my wishes come true."

I pull back. "I don't have a lot of nice things with me. Where are we going?"

"I'm not telling you."

"Then, how do I know what to wear?"

"You can go as you are."

I am wearing yoga pants and a T-shirt. I packed in a haze, worried about Charlotte and upset, and my suitcase is a mish-mash of uncoordinated outfits. "I don't think so."

Jamison rolls his eyes. "Casual. Wear whatever you want."

"Now you're giving me anxiety."

He grabs my hand, and walks me into the bedroom. Throwing my suitcase on the bed, he opens it then rummages through my clothes.

"What are you doing?"

"Finding you an outfit to wear so you aren't anxious."

"What if I had my vibrator stashed in there?" I seriously say.

"Didn't you kill the motor?" he teases.

Okay, I walked into that one.

"Nope. Not yet."

His eyes widen. "Is it in here?"

"No."

I don't know. I can't remember if I packed it or not.

He puts a pair of jeans on the bed, reaches into my suitcase behind him, and randomly picks a shirt. "This one."

"You didn't even look at it."

"Doesn't matter. You're going to look hot in it." He turns back to the suitcase. "On the other hand, you definitely need to wear these tonight." Jamison pulls out a black lace thong and matching push-up bra.

The man has seen me naked and made me orgasm so many times I lost count. He knows my vibrator's motor is about to die out. But heat still rises through my face.

He sits down on the bed. "You can change now." He waggles his eyebrows at me.

I slap his shoulder. "Go away."

"Can't blame me for trying." Standing up, he slaps me on the ass. "Don't take too long. You're already perfect."

7

Jamison

QUINN SPENDS TWENTY MINUTES GETTING READY. I HOP IN THE shower in one of the guest bathrooms and get done before she does. I'm waiting for her on the couch when my phone rings.

Valeria pops up on the screen.

"Hey, V," I answer.

"Jamison, how are you doing?"

I stand up and walk to the windows, staring out at the twinkling lights of Manhattan against the dark of the night. "I'm good. Everything okay?"

"Yes, darling. I'm good."

"Are you back in the country now?"

"No. Filming is going to take a little longer. I think I'll be stuck here another three weeks."

I run my hand through my hair. "Cindy with you?"

"She had to fly back for work."

"Everyone on the set treating you well?"

"Yeah. Everyone is very kind." She pauses.

"V, what is it?"

She lets out a big sigh. "My father."

My gut flips. "What about him?"

"He's coming to town and wants to see us."

"About what?"

"Honestly, Jamison, I have no clue. He said he wants to see us, and we both need to make time. I don't think I can hold him off any longer."

I let out a big breath of air. "When is he in town?"

"Next month. He's not sure of the exact date yet. I'm sorry to ask you this, but you know how he is."

Yep. You don't have to remind me how my father-in-law Alejandro Gómez is.

"Okay, V. Text me the date when you know. Also, I'm staying at Chase's penthouse while I remodel. I'm sure he'll be fine if you stay here while you're in town."

"Thanks, Jamison. And...I'm sorry to put you through all this."

"No worries, V. Glad you're all right."

"I do miss you though."

"I miss you, too."

The bedroom door opens. I turn as Quinn walks out. "I've gotta go. I have a hot date tonight."

"Go get 'em, Tiger."

"Talk soon. Bye." I hang up the phone and whistle at Quinn. "I told you that you would look hot."

She grimaces. Sorry. I didn't mean to interrupt your call."

"You didn't. Ready to go?"

"Yes."

I help her into her jacket, throw my own on, and we head for the private elevator in my wing. We step outside into a bitter-cold wind. I pull Quinn into me. "The restaurant is two blocks away. You good to walk, or is it too cold and windy?"

"I'm from Chicago. This isn't wind."

"Guess we are walking, then."

"Are you going to tell me where we are going?"

"First stop is the best burger in New York."

"Yes! I've been craving a burger all day. What's the next stop?"

"I'll tell you later."

"You're going to torture me," she whines.

"I have better ways of torturing you." I grin at her.

"Ha, ha."

It doesn't take long for us to get to the restaurant. It's a micro-brewery with over one hundred craft beers. Massive steel barrels rise from the bar floor to the ceiling. Several booths line the walls, and the rest of the restaurant is outfitted with tables and chairs.

The restaurant has customers, but it isn't packed.

"Jamison," the hostess says. "How've you been?"

"Good. Carrie, this is Quinn."

"Nice to meet you, Quinn."

"Same to you."

"Just you two?" she asks.

"Yes. Is there a wait?"

"I'll get you in. Come with me." She leads us through the bar and restaurant area to the booth in the back. "This work?"

"Perfect, Carrie. Thanks."

She sets down the menus and leaves. I help Quinn take off her coat and put it on the hook on the side of the booth then do the same with mine.

We sit across from each other.

"They have milkshakes here, but I think the beer is better," I tell her.

"Beer sounds good. What's good here?"

I squint. "Do you normally drink beer?"

"Not normally."

"Get the sampler, then."

"Good idea."

The waitress comes over, and I order two samplers. We each order a burger and fries, and she leaves.

"So, you were a paramedic with Chase, Noah, and Xander?"

"That's how Chase and I met Noah and Xander."

"You've known Chase the longest?"

"Yes. Who have you known the longest?"

"Piper."

"I like Piper. Still can't believe she dropped twenty-five G's on Noah's sorry ass."

"No way Piper was going to let that blonde win."

"She told you about the blonde?"

"No. She had Charlotte, Vivian, and I on FaceTime. We saw the entire show. It's how Charlotte bid on Xander."

So she saw me in a speedo, acting like a macho dickhead for the crowd. Awesome.

"You saw me on stage?" I wince. "Thanks for not holding that against me."

"What do you mean?"

"It's a pretty egotistical contest."

"Why do you do it, then?"

"For charity."

"You don't have fun doing it?"

"Not really. I have to drink a lot before I get up there."

Quinn laughs. "I think I would have to as well. But for the record, I thought you were pretty hot."

"Not really fair. You saw me, but I didn't get to see you."

The waitress sets two samplers down with six glasses of beer in each. "Need anything else?"

Quinn shakes her head. "No thanks."

"All set, thanks," I tell her and she leaves again.

Quinn picks up our conversation. "You're not a paramedic anymore, right?"

"I own an ambulance company with Chase and a few other investors." I leave out the fact I also own part of the restaurant we are sitting in, the company that makes the ice cream we licked off each other last night, and hundreds of other companies across the world.

"Was that a scary leap?"

"Going from being a paramedic to the owner?"

"Yes."

"I think for me it was having to make sure we had the best paramedics, reliable vehicles, technology, contracts with the hospitals, etc. People's lives are at stake, so the responsibility was bigger than when I was the one person going on one call. Now I'm responsible for making sure thousands of calls a day get answered and the attention they need."

She finally says, "That sounds like a scary leap to me."

"I suppose."

"What made you leap?"

"It was time. Noah had moved on. Xander was a doctor. Chase and I were running multiple crews for the company and saw ways we could expand and make things more efficient. When the opportunity came up, we took it. Then we started making our own opportunities by buying out the majority of the investors and keeping the ones we wanted on our team."

Her bright-blue eyes stare at me. "So, you just went for it?"

"Yep."

"Hmm."

"Tell me what kind of books you write."

She hesitates.

"Tell me," I urge her.

"I wrote a series of thrillers, a few romantic comedies, and I dabbled in urban fantasy for a bit."

She writes thrillers? No freaking way.

"You hid that little piece of information last night."

She takes a sip of beer and doesn't say anything.

"I want to read what you wrote."

"No way!"

"Why not? I love thrillers. Let me start with those."

"I'm not an author. I submitted my books. No one picked me up."

"So? One person read it and decided to give the book deal to a known name or some other story that resonated with them. It doesn't mean yours suck."

"Or maybe it does."

"Let me read it. I'll be the judge."

"Absolutely not."

"You won't let me read one?"

"No."

"What if I give you favors in exchange."

She tilts her head. "Do I even want to know what that means?"

"You pick. For every book you let me read, I'll owe you a favor."

Quinn peers at me. "Is this a sexual thing?"

I laugh. "No, but if you want that for your favor, I'm more than happy to oblige."

She rolls her eyes.

The waitress comes to our table and puts down our food. "Need anything else?"

"I'm good, thanks," Quinn says.

"I'm good, too. Thank you."

She leans over her burger and fries and inhales deeply. "Mmm."

"Wait till you taste it."

Quinn takes a bite, closes her eyes, and moans.

Jesus. This girl is killing me.

I stare at her.

"What?"

"You cannot moan in public like that."

"Why is that?"

"Because I'm trying to eat my burger, and my dick wants to escape out of my pants."

Her lips twitch.

"Glad I could amuse you with my suffering."

"Sorry."

We eat a few bites of our burgers.

"Do your mom and brother still live in the Chicago area?"

She swallows then takes a sip of beer. "My brother is a VP for an insurance company."

"What about your mom?"

Her voice lowers. "My mom is a personal assistant for a bigwig rich guy."

"Why do I get the feeling you don't like that?"

"I don't. He's been good to my mom—to our family. He helped my brother get his job. He pays my mom well enough, I guess."

"But?"

She shifts uncomfortably. "Is it okay if we don't talk about this?"

What is so bad she doesn't want to talk about?

"Sure."

"Thanks." She downs the rest of her beer and stares at the empty glass.

What spooked her? Is it her mom? This bigwig?

An uncomfortable silence follows. I want to see Quinn happy. Right now, she looks sad and borderline upset.

"Do you still see your cousin a lot?"

She smirks. "Funny. I should never have told you that."

I throw my hands in the air. "What?"

She changes the subject. "Where is your apartment compared to here? Is it close?"

"It's not too far."

"What are you doing to it?"

Ah. There's that smile.

"Updating it. It's all cosmetic."

"Have you lived there long?"

"I bought it five years ago."

"What made you buy it?"

"I got a good deal and loved the location. Do you live in the city or on the outskirts?"

"Near downtown. I rent though. I don't think I'll ever be able to afford anything in the city on my editor's salary."

"Maybe that's why you should publish your books." I wiggle my eyebrows.

"You seem really interested in my unpublished, unread books."

"I think it's cool you write. I couldn't do that. And they are only unread because you haven't put them out there."

She rolls her eyes again.

"Besides, I said I wanted to read them."

"I'll think about it."

I grin at her. "Yeah?"

"I said I'll think about it, not that you can," she reiterates.

"Think yes."

The waitress comes over. "Are you finished or still working on that?" she asks Quinn.

"I'm done. Thank you." Quinn hands her plate to the waitress.

"Quinn, you want a milkshake?" I ask.

"I'm stuffed."

I turn toward the waitress. "Can we get our check?"

"Sure." I hand her my card, she pulls out her card reader, and we complete the transaction. The waitress leaves.

"Ready?" I ask Quinn.

"Yes. Where are you taking me next?"

"I can't tell you. I just have to show you."

8

Quinn

JAMISON AND I LEAVE THE BAR. HE PULLS ME CLOSE AS BEFORE, BUT instead of sinking into him and feeling happy, I can't get my mom and Maximillion Evinrude, her boss, off my mind.

I hate that nasty man. *Even his name is pompous.*

"Quinn?" Jamison asks.

"Oh, sorry. What was that?"

Focus Quinn. Don't let Maximillion ruin your date.

"I asked if your boss got back to you? You said today you were worried about it."

"Oh. Yes. Everything is fine. He said to take a few days, and then I could do some work from here if needed. But I didn't bring my laptop."

"You can use mine if you want."

"Thanks. I've been saving for a new Mac. I suppose I should take the plunge and get it now. Everything is on the cloud, so I can access it anywhere."

"I got the new model the other day. It's pretty awesome if you want to try it out."

"Thanks, but that's out of my budget. I'll be sticking with a basic bottom-line refurbished one," I say in a teasing tone, but there is no joking about it. My salary doesn't go very far, living in the city.

"Well, feel free to use mine while you are here."

"Thanks."

"How long do you think you'll stay?"

"I don't know. I've never had this happen to any of my friends before. My boss sounded nice in the email, but he's only going to be nice for so long. He's a half dick."

"A half dick?"

"Yeah. Sometimes he's a dick and sometimes he's not. It's like Jekyll and Hyde."

"Glad I could learn a new term tonight. We're here." He waves me ahead of him.

I open the door and stop.

Jamison puts his arms around my waist from behind and leans into my ear. "You have to step all the way in for me to come in as well."

"Oh, sorry." I move in and to the side then I survey the busy room. There's soft music playing and a coffee bar. Tables, couches, and comfy chairs are scattered throughout, and people are drinking coffee and reading or chatting. A few people are quickly typing on their laptops. Bookcases line every wall, full of novels. "You brought me to a bookstore?"

He grins at me. *The* bookstore."

"*The* bookstore?"

He points to all the shelves. "These are all books by indie authors."

"All of them?"

"Yep."

Jamison glances at his watch and grabs my hand. "Come on. We're going to be late."

"For what?"

"The event."

He guides me through the store and into another room where there are tables and chairs similar to the store, and pads of paper and pens are scattered.

"Jamison. You decide to start writing?" A woman with pink-rimmed glasses and black hair asks him.

"Nope. Still no talent. But I did bring someone who does. Kim, meet Quinn. Quinn, meet Kim. She's published a few series and has several pen names."

Kim stands up and shakes my hand. "Quinn, nice to meet you. How long have you been writing?"

My initial reaction is to run and hide. I'm going to kill Jamison.

"I haven't published anything," I quickly say, my face heating up.

"You're in the right place, then."

"I don't understand."

"Kim writes full-time and also leads a discussion on how to self-publish, market, and find resources based on your genre. She also moderates a big community of writers on social media. She's a huge advocate in the indie community," Jamison tells me.

Wow. How does she do all that?

"Quinn, how long have you been writing?" she asks.

I take a deep breath. "Since I was twelve."

She puts her arm around my back, leading me over to a chair. "Have a seat. Tell me about your writing."

"There isn't a lot to tell."

"She wrote a series of thrillers, a few romantic comedies, and dabbled in urban fantasy," Jamison says with excitement.

Jeez. Did he record our conversation?

"You're a multifaceted writer. That's great!" Kim pats my hand.

"She is!" Jamison beams.

I furrow my brow. *This is super embarrassing.*

"What do you do for a living?" Kim ask.

"I work for a large publisher in Chicago. I edit romance novels."

"Ah. I see. Do you like it?"

"Well enough."

"You enjoy everything you read?"

"Nope. Some of it doesn't seem that great, but the authors have big followings, so anything they write, the publisher will look at and normally contract."

"What is stopping you from publishing?" Kim asks me.

Heat flushes my cheeks. "I got tired of getting rejection letters and realized I didn't have the talent."

Kim furrows her brow. "Rejection letters are an opinion of one person. Some of the biggest authors out there were rejected over and over and then got picked up by the traditional publishers only once they self-published and grew a large following. Did you stop writing?"

"No."

"Good. Don't."

I tap my foot.

"Do you want to know how to self-publish?"

"I never considered it."

"Can I ask why?"

Crap. What am I going to say to her? I can't tell her the truth.

"Let me guess. Everyone you work with says that the indie community is for those who aren't real authors?"

I wince.

"It's okay. We've all heard it. Can I show you something?"

"Sure."

She grabs an iPad from the table and brings up a screen. "This is the online community of authors I moderate. You are welcome to join. We discuss all kinds of topics, and everyone helps each other out." She pulls up the member list and taps on a dozen names. "Do you know what these authors all have in common?"

"They self-publish."

"Yes, but they also turned down major six or seven-figure publishing deals from traditional publishers."

I gape. "Why would they do that?"

"They are already making that kind of income and can control the process and quality of their work. Instead of a traditional publisher telling them what they can and can't do, they can get out to their readers what they want."

Hmm. That makes sense. Based on my knowledge from my employment, I know what she is describing is accurate. I'd seen many books bought from authors only to see them shelved and never published.

"But there are a lot of moving pieces to a book."

"There are. But once you publish a few books, you'll get a process down. You'll learn to streamline the different pieces. You can also hire things out."

I snort. "I won't be hiring anyone on my editor's salary."

"You can do that once your book income grows."

Is this really something I should consider?

But your work isn't good enough, Quinn.

"Have you ever had your novels beta read?" she asks me.

"No. No one has read them except the publishers I submitted my work to."

"No one? Not even Piper?" Jamison asks.

I shake my head.

"I think you'll find that if you get a few good beta readers, you'll get a good grasp of what others think about your writing. You may find that your work is better than you think. I'm sure you know this from your current editor experience, but good beta readers know your genre and will give you constructive criticism so you can fix holes in your story before publishing."

A man approaches us. "Sorry to interrupt, but it's time to start."

Kim smiles at me and hands me a card. "I hope you're staying. Here's my card. I would love to connect with you and help you get your stories out into the world. Contact me anytime."

I smile back at her. "Thank you. That's very nice of you to offer." I slide the card into my purse pocket.

She pats my shoulder and moves to the front of the room.

Jamison puts his arm around me and grins.

Yep, there's the cocky look I expected to see on him before I ever met him.

I try to concentrate on Kim. I can't believe he brought me here. I don't know why he is pushing this on me. I tried in the past and failed, and I don't need to keep repeating that.

Kim spends the next hour, leading a discussion on how to get started in the indie community. Several other authors add their input as well. Jamison seems to know most of them and has read many of their books.

Can their books really be that good?

Wow, Quinn, you've officially become a publishing snob.

It hits me in the face. I'm judging these authors before I even give them a chance. And from what Kim is saying, these authors are producing more work than they would be if they were picked up by a traditional publisher.

Hmm.

Several newer authors stand up and talk about some issues they are facing. The experienced authors give them suggestions and offer to help them outside the meeting.

Everyone is so nice and helpful. I didn't expect that.

I take a few notes on some points that stand out to me, and, when it's done, Jamison and I say our goodbyes to Kim and head back out to the store area.

Jamison's eyes shine bright. "Well? What do you think?"

I cautiously say, "It was interesting. Kim is nice. So were the others. They genuinely seemed to want to help each other out, which surprised me."

"Why?"

"It's pretty cutthroat where I work."

He grabs my hand and guides me over to the thriller section. "Let's pick some books."

"Okay. But I'm not familiar with any of these authors."

He spends a few minutes looking at the novels and selects several off the shelf. "Start with these."

"Why these?"

"All four of those authors write very differently, and they are my top four picks."

I check out the covers and read the back. "They sound interesting. I like the covers, too."

"My friend is a designer. He created that one."

"Wow. He's talented."

"He used to work for a big publisher here in New York, but he started his own company."

"That's awesome."

"Yeah. You should meet him sometime."

"During one of my many trips to New York," I tease.

"We can easily fix that problem."

What does that mean?

I'm not sure what to say.

He kisses my forehead and takes the books out of my hands. "Come on."

I follow him to the front of the store, and he reaches for his wallet.

"I can buy those," I tell him.

"No," he says, enunciating the N and handing the cashier his card. "My treat."

"Thank you."

"You're welcome." He finishes the transaction and takes the bag from the cashier.

We're walking back from the bookstore when he says, "So? Do you think you want to give it a try?"

"Yes. I'll read the books."

"That's not what I meant."

I stop walking. *Wait. Does he mean give us a try?*

Time lapses.

"Do you think you want to give self-publishing a try?"

My heart falls.

I sigh. "Why are you pushing this on me?"

His green eyes intensely stare at me. "You said it was your dream."

My pulse picks up. My mother's voice floats through my head. *"Dreams only disappoint and set you up for more heartache. Be realistic, Quinn."*

"Life isn't a fairy tale. I live in reality."

"Maybe you should add the opportunity piece into your reality."

Anger flares through my bones. "What does that mean?"

He holds his hands up. "I'm just trying to tell you that you have to create your reality. Forge your own path. Not stay stuck."

Stuck?

"Now you're judging me? You don't even know me," I accuse.

"No. I'm not judging you. You said you don't love what you do. You said you wanted to write."

"That's funny. It seems to me you're judging me."

"No, I'm—"

"I'm done with this conversation." I spin and walk away.

"Quinn!"

I blink back tears as I go.

He grabs my arm, and I shake out of his grasp. "Don't touch me."

"Quinn, stop, please!"

Tears are falling down my face. I swipe at my cheeks and speed up my walking.

"Quinn, I'm sorry. I didn't mean—"

I spin toward him. "Stop talking. Please," I cry out.

Pain crosses his face. I turn and continue on.

"Turn left at the corner."

I nod.

We walk the rest of the way in silence.

How dare he judge me. I've had enough disappointments and rejections in my life. I don't need any more. I work hard, am good at what I do, and support myself. I'm doing what you're supposed to do.

My mother's voice is once again in my head. "Be sensible, Quinn. Get a job, pay your bills, and stop living in la-la land," along with, *"Stop trying to be something you aren't. Stop setting yourself up to only fail."*

Then there's my brother's voice when the last rejection letter came. *"The experts have spoken. Stop spending your time on things that aren't going to happen and focus on sharpening your skills that are going to pay the bills."*

We are about a block from the penthouse when Jamison quietly says, "Quinn, I'm sorry. I didn't mean to overstep. I just think if you tried—"

I spin. "Do you know what it's like to constantly be rejected? You don't know me. You don't know what my reality is. So stop trying to convince me something can be that can't," I cry out with tears streaming down my face.

He tries to pull me into him, but I don't let him. I move as quickly as I can and get into the building. I throw my ID card at the security man and wipe my face.

The security man motions for me to go through, and Jamison puts his thumb on the gate pad scanner.

There is an uncomfortable silence as we wait for the elevator to arrive. When the doors open, the passengers get off, and we get on, along with four other people.

We say nothing. I stand next to Jamison, and he takes my hand. I close my eyes. The elevator stops on several floors, and we eventually are alone.

He turns into me. I have nowhere to go. I stare at his chest, but he tilts my chin up so I have to face him. His eyes are full of remorse. "I'm sorry. I would never intentionally hurt you. And I wasn't trying to judge you. You're the first person I've liked in a long time. I think you're amazing, and I'm already dreading when you leave."

My heart softens. *He thinks I'm amazing? He's dreading when I leave?*

"Can you forgive me?"

"Yes. I'm sorry for my outburst."

"No apology needed." He bends down, and his mouth grazes mine, soft and supple.

I wrap my hands around his head, and part my lips for him, slowly exploring his mouth as he pulls me as tight to his body as possible.

The elevator dings and doors open. We continue kissing, and they shut.

"We have to get out," I murmur against his lips.

"Mm-hmm," he replies but keeps kissing me and hits a button.

The doors open, and he walks backward, with me attached to his lips, into his apartment.

I forget about our fight and sink further and further into him. Wanting him, not knowing how it could be possible, but feeling that maybe we can figure out how to be together for the long haul.

I know better. I should see that this is just another unobtainable fairy tale and not set myself up, once again, for failure.

9

Jamison

XANDER WOKE UP A FEW DAYS AGO, AND HE CAN'T REMEMBER THE last twelve years of his life. He thinks he's still with Billie, his ex-girlfriend, and doesn't remember Charlotte.

We've been at the hospital all day. Charlotte is getting discharged and will stay at Noah and Piper's in New York until she can take care of herself. She is going to need a lot of therapy and a nurse to help during the day.

Piper finally tells her that Xander has been awake but doesn't remember her. She insists on seeing him, thinking he will recognize her, and we all hold out hope, but he doesn't. He's obsessed with Billie, and it's heartbreaking to see both of them so distraught.

Charlotte leaves with Noah and Piper. Quinn and Vivian ask if she wants them to come over and visit, but she says she wants to be by herself and rest.

I'm secretly happy Charlotte doesn't want them to go. It's my last night with Quinn in town. I haven't slept in my bed without her the entire time she's been here. And I don't want to. It's Saturday night, and she's leaving tomorrow so she can get back to work.

After our first date where I royally screwed up, I want to redeem myself. We've stayed in since then. I'm still kicking myself that I interfered in Quinn's business. I wanted to show her what was possible, but instead, I made her feel bad. I don't know her entire history, but I can see she's hurting and scared of something. I wish I could fix whatever is wrong, but I don't delve any further. I don't want to make her feel worse.

We've spent the week working side by side in the mornings. The day after our date fiasco, Quinn's boss sent her a nasty email about meeting her deadlines while she was gone. It's another reason I want to tell her to get her books published, but I bite my tongue.

I still want to read her stories, but I haven't asked again. I figure it's best if I stay away from the topic.

I work on my old laptop while Quinn works on my new one. She fought me on using it, and we finally pulled straws. Before we went to the hospital today, she finished up her project and closed the laptop. "I'm going to miss this computer."

"Keep it," I tell her.

"Funny."

"You can keep it. I'll get another one."

"Keep your brand new Mac? Are you crazy," she cries out.

I chuckle. "Seriously. Take it home with you."

"Ummm...no."

"No? Why not?"

She stands up, bends down, and kisses me on the forehead. "Thank you. It's very generous, but I'm not taking your laptop."

I wrap my arms around her waist. "Can I take you out tonight?"

"Let's see what's going on with Charlotte. I'm not sure if she's going to want us to come over to Piper's or not."

"All right."

"But you can if she doesn't want us to come over, and thank you for asking."

I stroke her cheek with the back of my hand. "Is there anything in particular you want to do before you leave?"

"Spend more time with you," she sweetly says, and my heart drops. I miss her already, and she's standing in my arms. I don't know where this is going between us, but I know that there is something special developing.

"I'm more than happy with that."

"We need to go, or we will be late."

We go to the hospital, the day progresses. All four of us are on an emotional roller coaster. On the way home, Vivian and Quinn are both upset about Charlotte. Chase and I are worried about Xander. Vivian is leaning into Chase's chest and Quinn mine.

Over the last week, we all act one way in the hospital, in front of the others, but as soon as we get into the car, it's as if we all can breathe. The pact we made the first morning the girls stayed with us was smart. It let everyone relax. There are no questions, explaining, or judgment from any of us, and we've naturally coupled off.

I don't know why Quinn cares, but she doesn't want it known to the others that anything is going on between us. She seems like a private person. I am, too, so I'm fine with it, but I wouldn't be hiding what's going on between us if she wasn't.

What's going on between us. For the millionth time this week, I wonder how to define Quinn's and my relationship.

I want more with her. I'm not sure how to make it work, but I know I want more. I think she does, too, but I can't be sure.

You need to tell her you want to see her again.

We could fly back and forth for a while. That could work. I have enough money for plane tickets and whatever else we need. Then we could see where it goes, and if it got serious, Quinn could move to New York and not work. She could focus on writing and launch her author career. I have plenty to support her. I could even pay for her to have an assistant to do all the parts of launching her novels she doesn't want to do.

The first step is to get Quinn to agree to see you after this trip. Don't upset her again. You did enough damage on your last date.

We are almost to Chase's place, and I murmur in her ear, "You want to go out tonight?"

"No thanks."

My gut drops. *Not a great sign that Quinn will agree to try out a long-distance relationship when you can't get her to go on a date.*

"Okay," I say, trying not to sound deflated.

She scooches closer to me and whispers, "Let's not deal with anyone else tonight." She pulls back and stares at me with her blue doe eyes.

My heart beats faster. I wink at her, and a small smile forms on her face, but she's also blinking back tears. I'm not sure if it's over Charlotte and Xander or if she's feeling as sad as I am about our situation. I kiss the top of her head.

When the car pulls up to the building, we get out and go directly into my apartment.

I sit on the couch and settle her on my lap. "I don't want you to leave."

Her eyes fill with water again. "I have to. I have to get back to my job, or I'll be fired."

I put my hand on her cheek. "There is something between us. This isn't just a physical thing."

She takes a deep breath and bites down on her lip.

"Quinn, tell me you want more from me."

She gulps. "How would it work?"

"I don't know, but we will figure it out."

Silence fills the room, minus the beating of my heart that I'm sure she can hear. She looks nervous, scared, and worried.

"Tell me what's running through your head, doll." I brush the hair off her face.

She puts her shaking hand on my cheek. "I want more from you, Jamison. But..."

"But what?"

"This doesn't sound realistic. Are we just setting ourselves up to fail and get hurt more?"

Shit. She's back to worrying about failing.

Words fly out of my mouth. "We don't know unless we try. Do you want it to be over between us?"

"No. Of course not."

"Just say yes, and let me take care of you."

"Take care of me?"

"Yes. Let me be your man, and I'll figure it all out. We can fly back and forth to start with and see where it goes. Then we can figure out the next steps."

"The next steps?"

"Yes."

She swallows hard.

I push my forehead to hers. "Tell me you want me to be your man."

"I want you to be my man," she whispers so quietly I hardly hear her.

"Good. Tell me you'll trust me to figure this out."

"I'll trust you to figure this out," she breathes.

"Good." I escape into the world I didn't know existed before Quinn. Crushing my lips against her trembling ones, I hold her tight to me, wanting to savor every part of her, knowing it's going to be hard with her so far away but having faith that whatever challenge is in front of us we can figure out.

I stand up with her in my arms, carry her into the bedroom, and lay her down. We quickly strip each other of our clothes, and when we're naked, she takes a condom off the nightstand, rolls it over me, and I pull her on top, wrapping my arms around her, so her warm flesh melts into mine.

Quinn straddles me and sinks, engulfing me in her heat. I groan as she moans, and digging my fingertips into her hips, rocking her slowly on me.

She sits up, closing her eyes as she takes more of me, inch by inch.

I don't know how I'm going to exist without her here, in my bed, every night. I already know it's going to feel empty. She feeds my body, my heart, my soul in ways I can't explain. I didn't know what I was missing before her, and now I do. There's no going back.

My beautiful doll rides me, shimmering against the dim light, her pert breasts slightly heaving, and her cheeks rosy with heat.

The sexiest woman on earth is mine.

"Oh..." she breaths, trembling into her first climax.

"That's it, doll," I tell her and bring my hand to the front of her, circling my thumb on her clit.

"Jamison," she whimpers, her mouth forming the O I'm going to be dreaming about when she's gone.

"Ride me however you want, doll," I pant, stroking her faster.

"Oh God...oh..." she cries out, spasming on my cock and throbbing against my thumb, which I know is only the first of her highs as her eyes roll back into her head.

I bring my hand to her back to support her as she trembles through her orgasm then back down to her hips when she's coming back down so I can thrust her faster on me.

"Come here," I tell her.

She leans down, and I swaddle her in my arms, crushing my lips to hers as she moans in my mouth.

"This is real, don't forget it," I say into her lips.

"I know," she whispers.

Her hips move faster on me, and her body clenches once more. "Oh God, Jamison," she cries out and convulses harder than the first time.

"I got you, doll," I murmur, thrusting into her harder.

"Oh..." She pushes her head in my neck, her warm breath panting.

I wish I could bottle her up and keep her like this.

Quinn unraveling is the most beautiful sight on earth. There's no worry or anxiety on her face. There's no hurt from whatever has happened in the past. It's just her: raw, uninhibited, impulsive.

Her mouth urgently finds mine, taking me further into our journey, heightening my endorphins, leaving no doubt I mean as much to her as she means to me.

As her body glides onto mine, my balls tighten, and blood scorches in my veins.

"One more time, doll?" I murmur to her.

"Mm-hmm," she whimpers.

"Oh fuuuuuuck," I groan as I unleash my mayhem inside her.

Our orgasms collide as I hold her tight, not knowing if it's her body or mine shaking.

When we come down, we collapse against each other. My chest is still heaving when she asks, "Can we keep this between us for a while?"

"You want to keep us a secret and hide?"

"No. I don't want all our friends in our business until we figure this out. It'll be easier for me without all their input."

I can understand that.

"Okay. Whatever you need, doll. As long as you're mine."

"I'm yours, Jamison."

10

Quinn

JAMISON CUPS MY FACE. "CALL ME WHEN YOU GET HOME."

"Okay." I'm blinking back tears.

I hate goodbyes.

He kisses me, and I want to stay in his arms forever. But I can't.

"Quinn, we have to go, or we won't get through security," Vivian insists.

Jamison presses his forehead to mine. "Have a safe flight." He kisses me one last time and pulls away. "You'd better go."

Vivian and I walk away from Jamison and Chase.

This sucks. How is this going to get any easier?

We don't say anything until we get through security and are having a coffee while we wait to board our plane.

"What's going on with you and Jamison?" she asks me.

"Our pact stays in place when we get home, right?"

"Of course."

"I don't want anyone to know anything."

"Okay. But what is happening with you two?"

"He said we would figure out how to make it work."

Vivian smiles. "That's great. You two are good together."

"But how is it going to work? This isn't realistic. I'm setting myself up to fail, but he asked me to trust him to figure it out."

"Then trust him."

I sigh. "I told him I would."

"Quinn, get your mom out of your head."

"How do you know she's in my head?"

"Because I know you. Jamison isn't your dad. You can take a bit of risk, you know. Everything doesn't have to be safe."

"So does that mean you had second thoughts and went for it with Chase?"

"Absolutely not."

I tilt my head. "You two looked pretty cozy all week."

"I'm not going to be one of his girls."

"How many does he have?" I cry out.

She shrugs. "No idea, but Meredith is Ms. Thursday."

I gape. "Chase has them assigned to days of the week?"

"Looks that way."

"Did he ask you to be one?"

"No, but he would have tried to get in my pants if I'd let him."

"But you seemed to like him."

She looks away.

I put my hand on hers. "I'm sorry. You really like him, don't you?"

"It doesn't matter. I'm not going to be one of his girls." Vivian looks at her watch. "We better go. They are boarding soon."

We go to our gate and shortly board. The plane ride home is quiet. Vivian and I are both lost in thought. It's early evening when I finally get to my apartment building.

I barely make it in the door when my buzzer rings.

"Delivery for Ms. Quinn Sinclair."

On a Sunday? What did I order?

I go downstairs to the lobby. A courier is waiting for me. I sign for the package. It's a box that's not super heavy but isn't just paperwork.

As soon as I get into my apartment, I open it and stare in shock.

A brand new Mac laptop with my name engraved on it and a pink cover is in the package.

Quinn,

You deserve nothing but the best. I miss you already. Thanks for making what should have been a shitty week, bright.

XOXO-

Jamison

PS - I still want to read your stories.

I STARE AT THE LAPTOP AGAIN AND THEN RE-READ THE NOTE several times.

I can't accept this.

I grab my phone out of my purse and call Jamison.

"Hey, doll. Did you get home okay?"

"Yes. Umm..."

"What's wrong?"

"I just got a delivery."

"Oh good, it arrived," he says like it isn't a big deal.

"Thank you, but I can't accept it."

"Why not?"

Why not? Where do I even start?

"For starters, it costs a few thousand dollars."

"So? It's my money, and I can choose what I want to spend it on. Or I should say *who* I want to spend it on."

"I'm going to return it. It's too much," I repeat.

"You can't return it. Your name is engraved on it."

I close my eyes. *Shit.*

"Jamison, you can't buy me expensive gifts."

My FaceTime app rings, and it's him. I accept it, and our call switches over.

"That's better," he says and smiles at me. "Hey."

I smile back. "Hey."

"Was your flight good?"

"It was fine. Let's get back to you not buying me expensive gifts."

"Why? Give me a good reason."

"Because it's too much."

"That isn't a reason."

I sigh in frustration.

"What's the real reason, Quinn?"

"I can't reciprocate with gifts like this."

"I don't want you to do anything of the sort."

"Well, it's not right."

"Says who?"

I'm not getting very far here.

"Can I tell you something?"

"What?"

"I have money. If I want to buy you something, I'm going to. Just say thank you, and don't analyze it. It makes me happy knowing you aren't working all day on a crappy computer."

"Jamison—"

"Shh. Let's talk about something else."

I take a deep breath.

"Did your motor run out yet?"

"Jamison!" I scold, trying to bite back a smile.

"Did you and Vivian decide when you're coming back to visit Charlotte?"

"Not yet. It won't be for several weeks." There is a knock. "Hold on a minute, someone is at my door."

"Okay, doll."

I look out the peephole to see who it is.

Why is Steven here?

"Steven, how did you get in?"

"Someone was leaving."

"Oh."

"Are you going to invite me in?"

"Sorry. Come in." I open the door and step back. "What are you doing here?"

"Who's that?" He points to the phone where Jamison's face is displayed.

I quickly say to Jamison, "I need to go. My brother is here."

"All right, doll. I'm glad you got home safe. Talk soon."

"Bye." I wave and hang up.

My brother raises his eyebrows. He has the same blue eyes and strawberry blond hair as I do. My friends all think he's hot, but he's so serious all the time about everything in life and working his way up the corporate ladder that I wonder if he'll ever get a girlfriend.

"A friend of mine."

"He called you doll."

I don't say anything, but heat flushes my cheeks.

Damn, my brother. Why can't he mind his own business?

"Who is he?"

"Just a friend I met in New York."

"This past week?"

"Yes."

"Why's he calling you doll if he's just a friend?"

"I'm thirty years old. Stop butting into my business and drilling me like I've done something wrong."

"Why aren't you answering my question?"

I need to get off the topic of Jamison.

"Why are you here? Everything okay with Mom?" My brother never just pops in.

"Mom's fine. How's Charlotte?"

"She'll be okay but has a long recovery ahead of her."

"I'm glad she is going to recover."

"Yes. So why are you here?"

"Wow. No love for me. You haven't even hugged me."

"Sorry, but you never stop in unannounced." I hug him.

"I was driving past and thought we should grab dinner. I haven't seen you in a while. You want to go?"

"You buying?"

Like I need to ask.

"With your salary, of course. Pick a place."

And there's the job jab.

"For that comment, I'm going to pick the most expensive place."

"I already made us a reservation at Kincaid's if you want to go there."

"I guess I can go there if you're going to make me," I tease him. Kincaid's is an upscale restaurant too costly for my budget, so I've only been there with my brother. "Let me go change. Make yourself at home."

"Okay."

I wheel my suitcase.

The Mac. I still can't believe Jamison bought me a top-of-the-line laptop. I want to be able to accept it graciously, but I'm not used to men buying me expensive items.

I open my suitcase to pull out my makeup, and the books Jamison bought on our date are on top. I had forgotten about those. We hadn't talked about the bookstore, and I hadn't seen the books after that night. There's a note on top.

QUINN,

Let's discuss after you read. I'm interested in what you think.

XOXO-

Jamison

PS - I'm still eagerly waiting to read your stories.

. . .

I ROLL MY EYES. NO ONE I KNOW HAS EVER READ ANYTHING I'VE written, but maybe I should let him read one so he can see that they aren't that good and stop bugging me?

I quickly change into a dress, put on my knee-high black boots, and freshen up my makeup and hair. "All ready," I chirp as I walk out of my bedroom.

Then I freeze. My brother is sitting at my table, with the note Jamison sent along with the laptop in his hand.

He glares. "You're sleeping with a guy you met less than a week ago?"

Blood rushes to my face.

"And he's buying you expensive presents?"

I'm paralyzed. I don't know what to say. I can't deny either of the things my brother is saying.

"You trying to end up in Mom's situation?"

How dare he.

I get over my shock of his questions and throw him some daggers of my own. Years of his warnings about not ending up like our mom, and all the guilt I always feel about what to do in relationships and what not to do come flying to the surface. This past week I've been happy. I was happy with Jamison, and I'm tired of living in the shadow of my mother's mistakes. But most of all, I'm tired of his constant judgments and unsolicited advice. "You don't know anything. Stay out of my business."

"You're making bad choices, Quinn. You don't know this guy, and you don't need a sugar daddy."

I've never done it before, but I slap my brother. Hard. My hand stings from the contact, and his cheek has a red mark.

He brings his hand to his face, and his eyes widen.

"Leave."

"Quinn—"

"No, Steven. Get out." I point to the door as tears well in my eyes.

"I'm trying to protect you. You don't know this guy, and I don't want you to end up heartbroken like Mom."

"Stop saying that," I yell. "I'm not Mom!"

"No, but you're making bad choices," he repeats.

"You don't know what choices I'm making."

"Oh yeah? What's this about your stories? Please tell me you aren't living in la-la land again with pipe dreams. It's bad enough you chose a career that doesn't pay you more."

"Do you ever listen to yourself? All you think about is money. And the only thing it has given you is the ability to be a miserable, lonely person."

He jerks his head back.

Silence surrounds us as both our assumptions about the other person are made clear.

"You're not my father," I quietly tell him.

"No, I'm not. But we know how he is, and at least I care enough to look out for you."

My heart softens. I sigh. "Steven, I know you love me and feel responsible for me, but I'm not your child. Just be my brother."

"I am being your brother. What do you know about this guy?"

"Enough."

"In less than a week, you know enough to sleep with him and accept expensive gifts?"

"It's not your business. Stop judging me."

"I'm not judging you. I'm trying to protect you."

"Stop trying. I'm an adult. I know what I'm doing."

"Do you, Quinn?" he says quietly.

"Yes."

"I hope you're right."

"It's my life. Worry about your own and stay out of mine."

Steven closes his eyes then opens them. "I think we should do dinner a different night."

"I agree."

He hands me the card that came with the Mac. "You've always been a good girl, Quinn. For your sake, I hope he's worth it."

My rage builds again. "A good girl? What does that even mean, Steven?"

"You've paid your bills. You've been in solid relationships. You've made sure you knew people before you slept with them."

"What do you know about who I've slept with and haven't? And where have those 'solid relationships' gotten me?"

"So far, not in Mom's situation."

"Stop. I'm so tired of having to pay for the sins of our mother. I'm not her."

"I didn't think so, but maybe you are."

I glare at him.

"I'll see you later, Quinn. Take care." He turns and walks out.

I sit down at the table, my insides shaking with anger, hurt, and millions of thoughts racing through my brain.

Slowly, I uncrumple my fist and re-read the card.

Steven isn't right. I'm not my mother, and I haven't done anything wrong. I know enough about Jamison, and I deserve to be happy.

It's time to stop living in my mother's mistakes.

I turn on the computer, connect it to my Internet, and pull up my Dropbox. Every story I've ever written is in there.

My favorite one, the first one of my favorite series, one that had been rejected years ago several times, that I've edited, rewritten, and edited again over the years, I hit the share button on.

I do a search for Jamison's company, and find his email, type it in the box. Then I write a message along with it.

JAMISON,

I forgot to say thank you.

I can't reciprocate by buying you something of equal value, but you keep asking me for this, so here it is.

XOXO-

Quinn

WITH MY HEART RACING AND MY PULSE BEATING HARD, I HIT SEND. It's time for me to trust that I know what I'm doing and trust in Jamison.

11

Jamison

HOLY SHIT. IT'S 4 A.M., AND I'VE NOT SLEPT. QUINN SENT ME HER book to read, and I couldn't put it down. My mind is spinning.

From a florist near her office, I order a dozen long-stemmed, pink roses, fill out the information online, and add a message for a card.

DOLL,

You are brilliant. I couldn't put it down. Please send me the next book.

Miss you.

XOXO-

Jamison

PS - This needs to get out in the world. I see this on film.

. . .

I PUNCH IN MY CREDIT CARD AND ALL THE OTHER INFORMATION and hit the submit button. Shutting my computer, I put it on the ottoman and enter the bedroom.

My eyes immediately go to the side Quinn slept on all week.

I need to see her again soon.

Throwing off my clothes, I crawl under the covers and switch pillows for the one Quinn used. It smells like her, and I inhale a few times.

She said that it would be a few weeks until she and Vivian were going to come out to visit Charlotte.

Make it happen. Create your own opportunities, Jamison.

I'm not going to sleep and decide to occupy my time with a video game, so I throw on a pair of shorts and a T-shirt. I walk out of my apartment and through the penthouse to the main room.

I'm surprised to find Chase already playing games. "You can't sleep, either?"

He pauses the game. "Nope."

"The game helping you get Vivian off your mind?"

"Nope."

I chuckle. "I'm glad you're awake."

"You happy to have someone beat your ass in person?" He throws the other controller at me.

"You wish. Anyway, what do you think about starting our conversations with the hospitals in Chicago? Instead of next month, what about next week?"

He slyly grins at me. "I think that's an excellent idea."

———

EARLY MORNING FRIDAY, CHASE AND I ARRIVE IN CHICAGO, AND AS soon as I turn my phone on, it rings.

"I have to take this, it's Valeria," I tell Chase.

"Go ahead."

"Hey, V. I'm just getting off a plane. Can I call you back?"

"I only have a minute. My father is coming into New York on Saturday, in two weeks. He wants to have dinner with us."

I sigh. I had forgotten about Alejandro for a brief moment. "Okay. Text me the time and place. Did he say what this is about?"

"No. He won't give me any hints."

"All right. I'll see you then. You want to stay with Chase and me while you are in town?"

"That would be great. Especially with my father in town."

"Good point. Okay, I'll see you then."

"Thanks for doing this, Jamison."

"No worries. I got your back."

"You always have. Thank you."

"Take care. See you in a few weeks." I hang up, stand, grab my bag from the overhead bin, and walk off the plane.

When we get into the terminal, Chase turns to me. "Valeria doing okay?"

"Yeah. Alejandro is coming to town and demanding dinner. V's going to stay with us while she's in New York."

He nods. "I take it if Alejandro is in town, then Cindy is staying in California?"

"That would be my guess. I think V is still out of the country on her shoot. I know Cindy went back to California for work."

Chase raises his eyebrow. "What does Alejandro want?"

I shake my head. "I have no idea. He isn't giving any hints."

"You need to figure out how to get away from that man."

"Gee, you think?"

"Sorry. I know we've gone round and round trying to come up with solutions."

"I'm pretty sure unless he dies or loses his memory, I'm never going to be free of him. And if he ever finds out about Valeria..."

Chase and I both sigh. Alejandro Gómez is not a nice or forgiving man. If he ever finds out about Valeria and my fake marriage, or that she is a lesbian, there will be hell to pay. It was bad enough when he learned she didn't marry another Colombian.

How Valeria carries any of his DNA is a mystery to me.

Alejandro is a cold, callous man. A man involved in deep criminal activity throughout all of Colombia. His reign of terror sweeps silently and secretively across many countries in South America, and one thing you don't want to do is defy Alejandro.

If I had only known about him before I agreed to help Valeria out, I wouldn't have married her.

I had been stupid—young, dumb, and trying to be the hero. Valeria was in a horrible position. If she went back to Colombia, he would force her to marry one of his men, and her dreams of becoming an actress would be over.

Her life would be over.

When her friend suggested I marry her to solve her problem, I didn't think twice. At twenty years old, I didn't even analyze it.

Our marriage allowed her to stay in the United States. It stopped her father from marrying her off. It allowed her to live her life the way she dreamed instead of in hell, which is what going back to Colombia and into a forced marriage would be for her.

The plan involved a three, four-year-tops marriage. I'd had no intention of being married anytime soon, so I never saw the big deal. It was just a piece of paper in my mind that gave Valeria her freedom.

I had no idea it would take away mine.

Our plan backfired. When Alejandro found out we were married, he flew into New York and gave us a lecture on how sacred marriage was and then made me convert to Catholicism so we could have a proper wedding in Colombia.

I went along with it because the guy not only scared the wits out of my twenty-year-old self, but Valeria said there was no getting out of it. If we admitted the marriage was false, her father would tell the government so they could deport her back to Colombia. Then he could marry her off.

Alejandro flew my family and Chase, Noah, Xander, and Matt, another friend who we don't talk to anymore because he was sleeping with Chase's girlfriend, in for the wedding. We all had to stay at his house, which was an actual compound, complete with guards securing the perimeter with machine guns.

It was then I realized that I had gotten myself into a situation that was bigger than just a few-year commitment to help out a friend.

In Alejandro Gómez's family, you did not dare divorce.

So, fifteen years later, I'm still married to Valeria. We are good friends and love each other but not in a romantic way. Since day one, we have lived our separate lives, whether dwelling under the same roof or not.

And besides the kiss, after we said our nuptials two times, we've never done anything else.

Over the years, Valeria has become a well-known star. She's a leading actress in many feature films and has numerous modeling and sponsorship gigs. We have kept it under wraps that we are married and convinced her father that it's better for her career.

She lives in California with her girlfriend Cindy when she isn't working. Her father thinks she lives in New York with me. When she comes into town, she stays with me, but she's so busy, I see her a lot less than I used to.

The guys are all friends with her and know the situation. We all like Cindy as well.

Besides Alejandro Gómez, Valeria and I have both created our dream lives and are happy. We've made tons of money, have careers we love, and there is no drama. Both of us would do anything to protect or help the other out.

I've never told anyone I've dated about Valeria and my situation. There's never been anyone I've wanted to marry or even live with, so besides Chase, Noah, Xander, and Cindy, no one knows. It's too dangerous.

Valeria was with Cindy for two years before she told her about our situation.

As I'm walking out of the airport to get into the taxi, I have a feeling I've never had before.

You should tell Quinn.

Slow down. You've only known her a little over a week. You can't put Valeria in danger.

Until I know for sure where this is going with Quinn, I can't make any dumb moves like when I was twenty.

12

Quinn

It's Friday afternoon, and my boss called a staff meeting at 4:45 p.m.

Leave it to him to send us off for the weekend with positivity.

I walk into the conference room and sit in a chair next to my co-worker Tim.

He leans toward me. "What do you think he's going to yell at us about now?"

"No idea. You're guess is as good as mine."

Bill Atwood, nicknamed in the office behind his back as "Half Dick," struts into the conference room and slams some folders on the desk. "There's a mutiny on this ship."

Mutiny? Oh jeez. What is he talking about?

My expression probably resembles the confused miens of my co-workers. Half Dick also likes to talk in code words.

"Let's reiterate who is in charge of this ship. Quinn, who's the boss?"

Oh God. Not again.

"You are, Mr. Atwood."

"Congratulations. You know your place in this company. Lindsay will no longer be the Team manager. Quinn, since you seem to understand the hierarchy around here, you may take over her role."

Team manager. Oh no. No, no, no!

"Sir, that's very kind of you, but I don't feel I'm qualified for that position." Nor do I have any desire to be in management. And I don't want to be reporting to Half Dick any more than I already have to.

"Rule number one, which you should already know, is not to argue. You will start your new role on Monday. The novel you are currently working on will be reassigned."

"I'm not going to be allowed to edit anymore?"

"No. You will be leading your team and overseeing their work. Now, it's Friday, and I have plans. I expect you all here on time come Monday morning. Quinn, I'll email you your new compensation package." Half Dick walks out as everyone stares at me.

Tim winces. "Congratulations?"

My other co-workers mumble the same with sympathetic expressions. I put my face on my arms, which are on the table.

I hear chairs moving, and Tim pats me on the back.

"Have a good weekend, Quinn."

I don't even look up and give him a wave. "See you Monday." When I eventually look up, everyone is gone.

This is one of my worst employment nightmares. I do not have a management bone in my body.

I go to my office and grab my laptop and slide it into my bag. I put on my coat and make my way through the building.

This week has been a cluster of highs and lows. My brother and I haven't spoken. He texted me he wanted to talk, but I ignored him.

I snort. *My brother.* He would be happy about this horrible promotion I've somehow "earned."

The book I've been editing is with an egotistical author I want to kill. She's not taking any of my suggestions and keeps putting comments on my edits that I must not get her story. *No, it's just not that good,* I want to write. The fact she got a signing bonus even to write the story irks me. She's nothing like Kim or the other authors I met in New York.

At least you don't have to deal with her anymore.

Charlotte sounds depressed anytime I call her, and Piper can't deny it, so I'm worried about her.

Jamison, besides the pain of missing him, has been my happiness this week. On Monday morning, I got a surprise delivery of pink roses with a note that he loved my book and wanted to read the next one. Part of me wondered if he was telling me that so I didn't feel bad, but when I texted him to thank him for the flowers, he called me right away and went on and on about how awesome different parts of the book were.

Since he seemed to genuinely like it, I sent him book two. The next day I got another set of roses with a similar message, and he's now read five books. Well, I'm not sure about the fifth book because today is the only day I haven't gotten roses.

Hmm. Maybe that means he read it and didn't like it?

I'm lost in thought, telling myself to chill out, that maybe he hasn't read it and cursing myself for sending him any of my books because he probably didn't like it, when I turn the corner of the lobby.

Jamison is standing outside the security area, wearing a black suit, holding a pink bouquet of roses, a big grin on his face.

Damn, he looks good in that suit.

My heart flutters. I run over to him and leap into his arms. "What are you doing here?"

"Kiss first. Talk later."

He dips down and kisses me, and the fire and passion we had in New York is just as intense.

"Let's get out of here," he murmurs to me.

"Mm-hmm," I say, continuing to kiss him.

"I missed you."

"You're here."

"For you." He pulls back from the kiss and grabs my laptop bag. "Let's go." Putting his arm around my shoulders, he leads me out to a black private car that's waiting on the curb.

As soon as we get into the car, I ask him, "Why didn't you tell me you were coming?"

His green eyes twinkle. He removes his suit coat then pulls me onto his lap. "I wanted to surprise you."

I cup his face. "This was the best surprise ever. Thank you. Why are you wearing a suit?"

"I'm taking you out tonight somewhere nice."

"Do I get to change?"

"Yes. The driver is taking us to your place first."

I kiss him.

He pulls back. "How was your day?"

"Ugh. Don't ask."

"What's wrong, doll?"

"I got promoted to the team manager and no longer get to edit."

He tilts his head. "You got a promotion you didn't want?"

"Do I look like manager material to you?"

"You look to me like someone who can do anything you put your mind to."

"Thanks for the vote of confidence, but management is not for me."

"Then why did you take it?"

"I wasn't given a choice."

"Seriously?"

"Yep."

He pushes my hair back. "That's a screwed-up business model."

"But I get paid more," I sarcastically say.

He pecks me on the lips. "I'm sorry. Maybe this is happening to send you a sign that you should publish your books."

I tilt my head.

"Don't look at me like that. You're seriously talented. All five of the books you sent me are amazing."

So he did read the last one.

I bite my lip.

"You don't believe me, do you?"

I wince.

"Quinn, I'm not telling you that to make you feel good. I wouldn't lie to you. You're the real deal."

I've always had a hard time accepting compliments, but I quietly say, "Thanks."

"You want me to change the subject, don't you?"

"I do."

"Say no more." He leans in, slowly exploring my mouth, and my happiness meter shoots through the roof. I straddle him, and my dress bunches up. My knees are on both sides of his hips, touching the back of the seat, and the only thing between his growing erection and my sex that is grinding against him is his thin suit pants and my even thinner underwear.

A deep, throaty groan escapes his lips.

"I've never done it in a car before. I think we should," I whisper against his lips and pull to release his tie.

He groans again and pulls his wallet out while still kissing me, and I unbuckle his belt and release his pants. He pops his hips up, and we both shove his pants down. "It'll have to be quick."

"I can be quick. Can you?"

"I can be whatever you need, doll."

In a swift move, I pull my underwear to the side and slide onto him, for the first time ever taking all of him in right away.

I whimper in his arms, and sit still, as my body adjusts to his length and girth.

"Okay, doll?" he murmurs against my ear.

"Mm-hmm."

He kisses my jawline, and I begin to rock my hips on him.

"Oh...yes...ride me like that."

"Like this?" I circle my hips slightly faster on him.

"Yeah, doll," his low gravelly voice tells me.

How can he always feel so good?

He laces his hand through my hair and locks his lips to mine, as toe-curling tingles of warning roll through every inch, every cell, every atom that I possess.

His warm breath travels to my neck. His lips suck on my flesh. Clasping me tighter, his hands move my hips faster.

He is heaven. This has to be what heaven feels like.

It's as if our bodies were created to be together; fluidly grinding and gliding, perfectly pulsing and pressing, masterfully tasting and teasing.

The tide of heat crashes throughout my body, gripping and pulling me at the same time into a spasming high of euphoria.

"Jamison," I cry out, and he moves me even faster.

I dig my fingers into his shoulders while my body convulses against his.

"Oh God...oh God...oh God," I cry out as I continue to have so much adrenaline fly through my body, I see white.

"That's it," he growls.

Dizziness overpowers me, and I collapse against his chest, no longer able to hold myself up, vibrating against him.

With one more downward thrust of my hips, he pumps his seed hard in me.

He wraps his arms around me, stroking my back as our chests heave against the other.

The car has stopped, but I didn't notice when.

"I'm going to have to shower before we go out now." He grins at me.

"I think I need one, too."

"It's a good thing I made a later reservation, then." He wiggles his eyebrows.

I kiss him and slide to the side of him. We clean ourselves off and get dressed good enough to run into my apartment. He steps out of the car and pulls me out, into his chest, then kisses me.

Everything is perfect until we turn. My brother is standing on the top of my stairs, with his arms folded against his chest, glaring down at us.

"Crap," I mumble. My stomach twists.

"What's wrong?"

"That's my brother."

Jamison pulls me tighter to him. "Then introduce me."

His tie is off and shirt only half-buttoned, he's holding his blazer, and he has a freshly fucked look. We both smell like sex. I'm not sure how long we sat on the curb parked, but my guess is that the car was rocking and who knows how loud we were.

My brother is giving Jamison the death stare, and my gut is flipping.

Why is he here?

Jamison is walking toward my brother and leading me with him. I want to crawl in a hole.

My brother comes down the steps and meets us at the bottom.

"Steven, what are you doing here?"

His eyes are slits. "I came to apologize and make nice, but I see I've interrupted."

Jamison holds his hand out. "I'm Jamison. Nice to meet you."

Steven looks him up and down and ignores him. Turning back to me, he says, "I'll talk to you later, Quinn." He starts to walk away.

"Steven!" I snap.

He stops walking and slowly turns.

"You're being really rude right now. I haven't done anything wrong."

"Haven't you?" he bites back.

Jamison steps in front of me. "No, she hasn't."

Anger flares through Steven's face and he says through clenched teeth, "Listen, man, you're lucky I don't drop you to the ground right now. The only reason I'm not is that my sister is standing here."

"Steven!" I chastise him again.

Jamison focuses on me. "Quinn, please go inside."

"No."

"I want to talk to your brother. Please."

"I think that sounds like a good idea. Let's talk. Go inside, Quinn," Steven says.

"So you can fight? No."

"I'm not going to fight," Jamison says.

My brother agrees. "I won't, either. Go ahead, Quinn."

"I'm not a child."

"I want to talk to your brother alone. Please go inside. I know you aren't a child." Jamison strokes my cheek. "Please. Trust me."

"Fine." I walk over to my brother. "I'm going inside, but you better not fight."

"I won't."

"You've reached a new low, Steven."

"Likewise." He scowls.

With my heart racing, I turn and walk up the stairs. When I get to the top, I turn around. My brother is still scowling. Jamison waves me inside.

I walk inside and close the door, hoping to listen to what they say but not able to hear a word.

13

Jamison

THE LAST THING I WANT TO DO IS CAUSE ANY RIFT BETWEEN QUINN and her brother, but I'm not going to let him shame her.

"I think we got off on the wrong foot," I tell Steven.

"No, we haven't."

"What's your deal."

He steps closer to me. We're both close in height. He looks like he works out, so I'm guessing if we did get into a fight that it's going to be an even match. But I promised Quinn I wouldn't fight so I'm not going to.

"You screw my sister in a car, and you want to know what my deal is?"

"I'm sorry you saw that, but your sister is thirty years old."

"So that makes it okay for you to use Quinn like a prostitute?"

My head almost snaps off my neck. *Do not hit him. You promised Quinn.*

"Excuse me?"

"You heard me."

"Yeah, I heard you refer to your sister as a prostitute, and I'm reminding myself that I promised Quinn I wouldn't hurt you."

"You heard me right."

Is this guy for real? Stay calm.

"Why would you even put Quinn and prostitute in the same sentence?"

"You need me to spell it out for you?" he bites out.

"Yeah. I do."

"You know my sister for a week, take advantage of her, send her expensive gifts, then roll up in here in a private car while fucking her in it. If that isn't prostitution, I don't know what is."

You've got to be kidding me.

I step closer to him. "What your sister and I do is none of your business. What I buy your sister is none of your business. For your information, I like your sister and am serious about her. And—"

"You're serious about my sister after a week?"

"Yeah, I am. Why do you find that so hard to believe? Quinn is an amazing person."

"Yes, she is. She doesn't need you to promise her the world only to let her down. She doesn't need to be your plaything you shower in gifts."

My pulse increases. "My intentions with your sister are nothing of the sort."

"I know your kind—"

"Your kind? What the fuck does that mean, Steven?"

He snorts. "Turn innocent girls into your toys only to break them. Go back to New York and leave my sister alone."

"You think I want to break your sister?"

"Don't you?"

"This is the last thing I'm going to say. I respect, admire, and adore your sister. I wouldn't do anything to harm her. Whatever I buy her is a gift because I want to, not because I expect anything from her in return. She's an adult, and anything we do is consensual and between us. And I won't be going back to New York and leaving your sister alone. Hopefully, one day, you and I can put this conversation behind us, for Quinn's sake. But if I ever hear you refer to her as a prostitute again, I will beat you until one of us is dead."

Steven doesn't flinch. "Is that so?"

"Yeah. Have a good night, Steven." I turn and walk up the stairs then knock on the door. Quinn opens it. Steven shakes his head, turns, and leaves.

I grab Quinn around the waist and lead her toward the elevator. "Let's go to your apartment."

When we get inside, she asks, "Are you going to tell me what was said?"

"No."

"Jamison!"

I turn her into me. "You know you haven't done anything wrong, right?"

She looks at me like she isn't sure if she has or hasn't.

"Quinn? What do you think you've done wrong?"

She blinks back tears.

I pull her onto my lap. "Tell me what's going on, doll."

"I didn't exactly tell you the entire story about my family."

I stroke her hair. "That's okay. Will you tell me now?"

She hesitates but then says, "I found out when I was eighteen who he was."

"He?"

"My father."

"All right. Who is he?"

She gulps. "Maximillion Evinrude."

"*The* Maximillion Evinrude?"

"Yes," she whispers.

Holy shit. Maximillion Evinrude is a one-hit-wonder famous actor turned politician. He's the governor of Illinois.

I kiss her forehead and wait for her to tell me more.

"My mother had a one-night stand with him and had my brother. He wouldn't marry her, but they moved in together. But he had another family she didn't know about. Then, when I was six months old, he left and took his other family to California with him to pursue his acting career. When he came back to Illinois, he hired my mother as a personal assistant, and they've been carrying on their affair ever since. My mother has never been able to move on with her life. He keeps sucking her back in. He showers her with expensive gifts, which always makes her go back to him."

"Ah. So that's why you had a hard time accepting the laptop."

"Yes. My mom knows she shouldn't be with him, but she can't stop. She's still his mistress. And all she ever told me was, 'Don't be easy, or you'll never be anything more to a man than sex.' "She looks away, and her face flushes.

So this is why her brother thinks what he does.

I cup her face in my hands. "Quinn, you don't believe I think you're easy, do you?"

She furrows her brows. "I don't know. We had sex the first night we met."

"Yeah, we did. That doesn't make you easy."

"Quinn, do you regret our week together?"

"No," she whispers.

"Good. You know you're more to me than sex, right?"

She nods, but I don't think she truly believes it.

"Quinn, I adore you. I couldn't stand being away from you. You mean more to me than just sex."

A tear drips down her cheek. "I know."

"Do you?"

"Yes."

"You haven't done anything wrong. You're thirty years old, and we're consenting adults."

Another tear falls on her cheek.

I wipe it away with my thumb and peck her on the lips.

How much guilt is she feeling, when she shouldn't be feeling any?

I wrap my arms around her and hold her. She snuggles into the curve of my neck.

"What we have is real. It's new, but it doesn't mean it's not real," I tell her.

She nods into my neck.

"Is this why you didn't want anyone to know about us when we were in New York?"

"Yes."

"You thought they might think you were easy?"

"Yes."

I pull her tighter to me and sigh. "And why you don't want them to know right now?"

She pulls back from me. "No. I meant it when I said that until we figure it out, I don't want their advice. It's not their business and only ours."

"All right, doll."

"Are you still okay with that?"

"Yes. Of course. I told you, as long as you're mine."

"I'm yours. I only want to be yours."

"Good. Because I'm only yours."

14

Quinn

VIVIAN AND I ARE FLYING INTO JFK. I HAVEN'T SEEN JAMISON since he surprised me in Chicago a few weeks ago. We talk daily. He sends me flowers every day at work, which helps brighten my day since I hate the new position my boss promoted me to. I told him he doesn't have to, but he keeps sending them.

He's read almost all my manuscripts. I only have a few more to send him. Every time he reads one, he tells me how amazing it is and all the things he thought about it.

Jamison keeps encouraging me to publish my novels, and I'm slowly growing the confidence to look into it a bit more. I reached out to Kim, and we are meeting up for coffee while I'm in town so I can ask her some questions. I also joined her social media group and have been interacting with some authors.

Since no one besides Vivian and Chase know Jamison and I are together, Piper is insisting we stay at her place. I'm trying to figure out how to stay at Jamison's without anyone figuring out we're together, but nothing is coming to my mind.

We left on a six o'clock flight since my boss won't let me have any time off right now. It's around nine o'clock, and Noah said he would send his driver to get us. Vivian and I are on the escalator going to the ground level when we see Jamison and Chase waiting for us.

Jamison and Chase pick Vivian and me up when they hug us.

"Chase, what's wrong with your face? It looks bruised." Vivian cups his cheeks.

The guys look at each other uncomfortably.

"What?" I ask Jamison.

"Xander gave Chase a nose punch for his birthday."

"It was your birthday, and he punched you?" Vivian cries.

"Nope. It was his birthday, and he punched me."

"Why did he punch you?" I ask him.

Silence.

Jamison finally says, "Xander thought he saw Billie. He didn't and freaked, and we had all been drinking a lot. Everyone is fine. It's water under the bridge now."

Vivian and I exchange a look. *So he's still not over Billie. Poor Charlotte.*

"What are you guys doing here? I thought Noah's driver was picking us up?" Vivian asks.

Chase has one of his cocky looks on his face. "Charlotte is wiped out from her therapy and took a pain pill. She's down for the count. Bennett flew in and needed to talk with Piper and Noah over dinner, so I told Noah we would get you and bring you to their place tomorrow."

I look at Jamison and smile.

"You look gorgeous. I missed you," he murmurs in my ear.

"I missed you." I kiss him.

"Okay, lovebirds. Let's get out of here. Ladies, you hungry?" Chase asks.

"I'm starving," Vivian says.

I nod. "I could eat."

Jamison grabs my bag.

"Great. Let's go have some fun, then." Chase grabs Vivian's bag.

We pile in Chase's car, and it's déjà vu of the previous trip to New York. Vivian and Chase, although Vivian swears nothing has happened between them, and Jamison and me.

I'm cuddled up on Jamison's chest, and everything feels perfect. I inhale his clean, woody scent. He kisses the top of my head and winks.

We pull up to a restaurant not far from Chase's place. There is a line out the door, but the guys steer us directly to the front, and we get right in.

"Well, aren't you two important around here," I tease them.

"Real VIPs," Vivian digs further.

Chase leans down and whispers something in Vivian's ear, and she slaps him on the biceps. Jamison just smiles.

"You're awfully quiet tonight," I say to him.

"It's been a long week."

I put my hand on the side of his head. "Everything okay?"

"Perfect. You're here." He gives me a quick peck.

The hostess takes us to a booth near the back.

"Thanks for having us stay again, Chase," I say.

"You're not staying at my place. Unless you want to."

"I'm not?"

"My place is finished. The movers moved my stuff back in today," Jamison says. "Assuming you're coming with me?"

I laugh. "I better be."

"So... I'm staying at Jamison's?" Vivian asks.

"No. You're staying at my place. Unless you aren't comfortable doing that?" Chase raises an eyebrow.

She hesitates for a moment. "That's fine. Thank you."

"No thanks needed," he tells her.

She sits back on her seat and takes a sip of water.

The waitress comes over, and we order drinks. Vivian and I drink wine, and the guys each have a beer.

"What's good here?" I ask.

"Everything," Jamison says.

"Quinn, you want to split nachos?" Vivian asks me.

"Sounds good." I put my menu down.

"If you're going to do that, then we should just get a bunch of appetizers to split," Chase says.

"Who says we'll share our nachos?" Vivian asks.

Chase leans in and whispers something in Vivian's ear, and she elbows him.

"We are not sharing the nachos, then."

Chase pretends to stab himself in the chest.

Jamison's phone rings. He looks at it. "Sorry. I have to take this." He stands up and walks out of the restaurant."

I look at Chase. "Does Jamison seem stressed to you?"

He looks like he's about to say something but smiles. "Long week."

"Is that it?"

Chase changes the subject. "How's your new position, Quinn? Jamison said, you got a promotion you didn't want?"

"I did, and it's horrible."

"Did you start looking for a new job yet?" Vivian asks.

"No."

"Why not?"

"I doubt I'm going to find anything in this job market. Especially with my industry the way it is now."

"Jamison said you wrote some awesome stories. Why don't you publish them?" Chase says.

He told him?

My face heats.

"Jamison read your stories?" Vivian asks, looking hurt. The girls have asked for years to read my stories, and I've never let them.

I can't believe Jamison told Chase.

"It's a long story," I tell her.

I decide changing the topic is best. I say the first thing that pops into my mind. "Where were you when Xander punched you?"

"In a restaurant."

"A restaurant," Vivian and I both cry out at the same time.

Chase chuckles. "Yep."

"The restaurant didn't call the cops?" Vivian asks.

"Oh no, they did," Chase says.

"Did you get arrested?"

Chase shakes his head. "We know the police officers who came, and we got lucky. Noah threw a wad of cash at the restaurant owner, who we knew, too."

"He threw a wad of cash at him?" I say in disgust.

"Yep."

Vivian chides, "Simmer down, Quinn."

"What?" I ask.

"I'm sure things got broken."

"Unfortunately, there were," Chase admits. "It's not like we're proud of what happened."

"Of course you aren't." Vivian rushes to his defense.

Jamison slides next to me. "What did I miss?"

"Xander's birthday," Chase tells him.

Jamison groans. "Let's not talk about that. He's had better days."

"Xander! What about Chase?" Vivian points to his face.

"You embarrassed to be seen in public with me like this?" Chase teases her.

"Funny," she says.

The waitress comes over and takes our order. Chase orders a bunch of appetizers for the table, including Vivian and my nachos.

Jamison looks to me. "You're spending the night at Piper's tomorrow, right?"

"We're supposed to be. I haven't figured anything else out," I say. I know I'm here to visit Charlotte, and I want to see her, but I want to stay with Jamison for the entire trip.

Why does he look relieved?

As quickly as it crosses his face, the expression leaves. "Xander has been depressed, and Noah said he thinks Charlotte is, too. I think it will be really good for her to be with all of you. Even if it's just for a night."

He is only being a good friend. Stop worrying, Quinn.

Jamison puts his arm around me, and the conversation continues. We eat and finish our drinks, but I can't help feeling that Jamison seems distracted.

We leave the restaurant. Chase and Vivian get dropped off first. When we're alone, I sit up and turn to him. "Is everything okay?"

"Yes, why?"

"You seem distracted. I feel like there is something you aren't telling me."

"I'm sorry—a lot of things going on. Everything's fine, doll. I'm happy to see you." He pulls me onto his lap.

"Is this a bad time for me to be here?" I ask quietly.

He brushes the hair off my face. "No. It's never a bad time for you to be here."

"Are you sure?"

"Yes. And don't ever question that."

I take a deep breath.

"Quinn, I want you here. All the time. I've missed you terribly."

"I've missed you terribly."

He rubs his thumb over my lips.

"Did you talk to your brother?"

"Ugh. Why do you have to bring that up?"

"Because I know it's been bothering you, and you love him. Did you meet up with him?"

"No."

"Why not?"

I look away. "I'm not ready to." What I don't tell him is that my brother and I had a long exchange of text messages that didn't result in anything good. He also had my mom call me to lecture me on how I shouldn't repeat the sins of her past and present.

All my brother and mother did was fuel the fire. I'm angry at them both. They have no right to assume Jamison and I are anything like my father or mother's situation.

The more I get to know Jamison, the more I'm falling for him. We talk, FaceTime, text, and email daily. While the flowers he sends every day are beautiful, what I love most are the cute and funny notes.

Jamison shows me he's always thinking of me. One day, I mentioned I was stuck in the office and starving but not leaving anytime soon, and he had lunch delivered. Another time, I was having an awful day. My boss was in one of his moods, and when I left work, a private driver was standing in the lobby with my name on a sign. He took me to a spa where I had a massage, facial, pedicure, and manicure.

There are so many ways he surprises me, and I stopped telling him to not spend money on me. He reminds me over and over that he told me the last night I was in New York he wanted to take care of me, and I realize that this is his way of doing it when we are apart.

I push all the guilt and voices of my mother and brother to the back of my head and keep reminding myself that I'm not my mother, and Jamison is not my father.

"Quinn, I don't want you not to have a relationship with your brother. He's had some time to calm down. Surely he's come to his senses by now."

I look away.

Jamison turns my face toward him. "You did talk to him, then?"

"Just through text."

"And?"

"I don't want to talk about it."

"Quinn—"

I put my fingers over his lips. "Can we just concentrate on you and me while I'm here and not anyone else? Our time is limited as it is."

He takes a deep breath. "Okay. We can discuss that later."

"Or never."

"Quinn!"

I sigh. "Okay, later." I lean in and brush my lips against his.

He wraps his arms around me tighter and palms my head, deepening our kiss.

I begin to shift my body on him when the car stops. "That was quick," I murmur against his lips.

"That's the last thing that's going to be quick tonight." He winks. We get out of the car, and he grabs my bag and leads me into the lobby. "Pull out your ID, doll."

I get out my identification card and hand it to the man at the front desk.

"Conroy, please give Quinn full access."

"Sure thing, Mr. Lancott."

I look at Jamison in question, but he just kisses the top of my head.

Conroy types something into the computer and hands me my card back. He points to a scanner box. "Please put your thumb on the screen and roll it like this," he instructs.

I follow his instructions.

"Thank you, Ms. Sinclair. You only need to press your thumb on that box by the gate from now on."

He doesn't want me announced before I come up?

"Thank you."

Jamison and I get through the security gate and into the elevator, and he punches in a code. It doesn't take long before the doors open.

"Wow." I'm taken aback by the view of the city, similar to the one Chase has but also different.

"Come on, doll." He holds my hand and guides me through the penthouse, giving me a tour.

"This is beautiful," I gush. It's an open floor plan with vaulted ceilings, modern grays, blues, and whites.

"You like it?"

"What's not to love? This is incredible." The entire skyline can be seen through floor-to-ceiling windows lining the wall.

He puts his arms around my waist, and I put mine around his shoulders.

"Do you think you could see yourself here?"

"It's beautiful," I repeat.

"But would you be comfortable here?"

"I think someone would be insane to be uncomfortable here."

He cups my face and brushes his thumbs on my cheeks. "Could you live here?"

My heart beats faster. *What exactly is he asking?*

"What do you mean?"

He takes a deep breath and gulps, staring into my eyes. "I miss you. I don't like being apart."

"I don't like being apart, either."

He puts his forehead against mine. "I love you."

He loves me. I already know I love him but I didn't expect him to tell me so soon.

I blink back tears. "I love you, too."

He kisses me. "Why don't you move to New York."

"Leave Chicago?" I cry out.

"Yes. We can go visit whenever you want."

Leave Chicago. Move to New York.

"Let's sit down." He pulls me over to the couch and onto his lap.

"What about my job?"

"You hate your job."

"Yeah, but it pays my bills."

"I'll pay your bills. You can focus on writing and getting your books published."

I jerk my head back. "What?"

"You don't have to worry about work. I'll take care of all the money."

"What? I can't not work."

"Why? Focus on your writing. Get your books published. They're incredible, and I'm not telling you that to be nice. You have talent, and you're wasting it working where you are."

What is he thinking?

"Thank you for believing in me, but honestly, you can't just pay all my bills."

"Yes, I can. I have more than enough money."

"This isn't about how much money you have."

He looks at the ceiling then back into my eyes. "Don't you want to be together. In the same city?"

"Of course. That's not it."

"Then what is it?"

"You can't bankroll me."

"You make it sound like I'm trying to do something horrible. I have the money...more than enough. You should be writing and not working at a job you hate. I want to be with you. All the time, not just here and there. What else is there?"

"My life in Chicago. My friends and family. I can't just up and move at the drop of a hat."

"Quinn, listen to me. I'll give you a credit card. You can fly in and out whenever you want. You won't ever have to ask for money or anything like that. You just use the card and do whatever it is you want to do. You can focus on your writing. We can be together. What objection could you possibly have with all of this? Unless you don't want to be with me?" His voice lowers a notch.

I lace my hands through his hair. "Jamison, being with you doesn't have anything to do with what I'm trying to tell you."

"Then what does? I don't understand. I have the money to make all this work."

"It's not about money."

Frustrated, he holds his hands in the air. "You don't make sense. You say it's not about the money or me, then what is the issue? I'm giving you the resources to fly back. I'm telling you whatever you need I'll give you. I don't understand."

What he's saying makes sense. I understand why he feels this way, but Chicago is all I've ever known.

I lean in and kiss him. "Look, I want to be with you. Every day, I want to be with you. I hate being apart."

"Then move to New York, and let's be together."

"I've never not supported myself."

"Because you had to. You don't have to anymore. I can do that."

I sigh. "Yes, I can see that, but this is a lot for me to take in. I need to wrap my head around it."

"You aren't saying no?"

"I'm not saying no. I didn't expect you to ask me to move in with you. This is a lot for me. Can you give me time and let me process this?"

He lets out a big breath. "Okay. I can give you time."

I stroke his cheek. "And it's an amazing offer. Thank you for being so generous."

"Quinn, if you move, whatever is mine will be yours. You don't have to thank me or feel like you're taking handouts."

Whatever is his will be mine? That sounds more like marriage to me, but that isn't what he's offering.

I should be elated. I should jump at the chance. I want to be with him more than anything. I want to share my life with him, but something is telling me to think things through.

My mother's words once again haunt me. "Never move in with a man unless you have a ring on your finger and you've said, 'I do.'"

15

Jamison

"Jamison, darling." Valeria pulls me in for a hug and kisses me on both cheeks.

"V, you look great. How was your flight?"

"Long. The usual." She steps back and surveys the penthouse. "Nice job on the remodel. It looks great."

"Thanks. It took long enough."

"Probably not as long as when they gutted it."

"True. Come in. Should we have a drink first?"

"If we have to deal with my father, then yes."

"Good call. I'll put your bag in your room. Grab me whatever you're having."

"Okay, darling."

I put Valeria's luggage in her room and come out to the main room. She hands me a glass of clear liquid. "Vodka tonic?"

"Yep. Going for the hard stuff."

I laugh and clink her glass. "Cheers."

We each take a mouthful and make our way to the sofas.

"What's new with you?" she asks.

"I'm in love," I blurt out.

"It's about time. Who is she?"

"Her name is Quinn. She lives in Chicago."

"Ah. I see. And are you moving there, or is she moving here?"

I sigh. "I want her to move here. I can't leave New York right now. We're going to be expanding in Chicago, but Chase needs to be on the ground, and I'm going to run things back here."

"Then have her move here."

I sit back and shake my head. "I asked her last night, but she won't."

"Why?"

"She said she needs some time to process it all."

"Does she love you, too?"

"She said she does, but she wasn't expecting me to ask her to move in."

"Then give her some time. It's a big move."

"I will. But I don't get what the issue is. I told Quinn she doesn't have to worry about money or working."

"You told her you would bankroll her?"

I groan. "That's what she called it."

"You definitely need to give her time to process that. Unless she's a gold digger, she is going to need time."

"She's not a gold digger."

"Well, there's your answer."

I sigh. I only want to be with Quinn. *What's the point of having all this money if I can't take care of the woman I love?*

"What did she say when you told her about us?"

"I haven't yet."

Valeria blinks. "Jamison, you need to tell her."

"She hasn't agreed to move in yet."

"You need to tell her before she agrees, not after."

"You didn't tell Cindy for two years and lived together most of that time."

"Yeah, and you saw how that almost broke us up."

"Two years is different than a month," I point out.

"Love involves trust, Jamison. Time doesn't matter."

I sigh again. I will tell Quinn, but I don't want to tell her if she isn't going to move here. I'm ready to share everything with her. There is no doubt how I feel about her or the life I want with her. Until she tells me she's sure about me, I don't want to risk our secret getting out. Not that I think Quinn would tell anyone, but I don't want to take any risks.

Valeria finishes her drink and looks at her watch. "You ready to face my father?"

"Ready as usual."

"I'm sorry again about this."

I hold my hand up. "Stop. It's fine. I signed up for this with you, remember?"

"No, I don't think you signed up for this."

"Till death do us part, twice, right?" I tease her and wink.

She looks at me sadly. "That's what I'm afraid of."

I know Cindy and Valeria want to get married legally, and now that the laws have changed, they could. I know Quinn is going to want that, and I wouldn't be opposed to it, but once I tell her, she will understand the situation, and I'll just have to make it up to her in other ways.

I throw back the rest of my drink and set it on the table. I reach to help Valeria up. "Come on. Let's not be late for your father."

———

ALEJANDRO HAS RESERVED A PRIVATE ROOM. IT'S A THREE-SIDED booth entirely enclosed by a door. No one can see in nor out, and we can talk freely with no one listening to a word. Besides the waitress, who Alejandro has instructed to knock before entering, the only other person in the room is his guard, who stands off to the side.

Typical Alejandro. Can't just eat in a restaurant like ordinary people. The intimidation factor is his usual method of operation and that includes with his family.

"Padre." Valeria embraces her father in a hug, and her Colombian accent comes out. She's worked hard to fit into American culture, and she's a talented actress, so I don't know if her smile is genuine or good acting.

I, on the other hand, have to work much harder. I smile as big as I can and embrace Alejandro, as my skin crawls. I detest the man.

"Sit," he commands us, motioning to the table.

We obey. There is no other option where Alejandro is concerned.

"Alejandro, what brings you to New York?" I ask him.

"Can't I come visit my daughter?"

Crap. I said the wrong thing right out of the gate. "I didn't mean—"

Valeria cuts in quickly. "Padre, you hate New York and haven't been here in years. What's the cause of this visit?" Unlike me, Valeria is comfortable standing up to her father.

He points at both of us. "I have to come to this godforsaken place because you two haven't been home in four years now."

Valeria and I both sigh.

"Padre, you know that my career has taken off. I've been working back to back on my movies and brand."

"Yes, what kind of husband lets his wife work this hard?" Alejandro glares at me.

"Sir—"

"Padre, you know Jamison supports me and my choices. I decided to work. My career won't be forever. You know how fickle Hollywood is."

"You won't be able to have a baby forever, either."

So, it's about this again.

"I told you, I don't want kids. Nothing has changed," Valeria adamantly says.

"What Colombian girl doesn't want babies? I'm ready for you to have babies."

Valeria shakes her head at him. I put my hand on her leg to remind her to calm down. She takes a deep breath. "Padre, Jamison and I are not having children. There is no further discussion on this. I'm sorry you flew to New York to discuss something that is never happening."

"That's not why I came."

"No?" Her eyes widen, and my heart rate picks up.

Great. There is something else.

"If you can't tell, I'm getting older."

"You do have all gray hair now," she teases him.

He focuses a hard look on me. "My only legitimate child is Valeria."

Yes, I know you screwed lots of women, and Valeria is the only child from your actual marriage. You don't need to remind me. I learned of Valeria's half-siblings when they were paraded around at the wedding, and on visits we used to have to make. I always felt bad for her mother, who had to sit through it all.

"Why are you bringing this up, Padre?" Valeria snaps.

Alejandro sits back. "Watch your tone."

I squeeze her thigh under the table, and she takes another deep breath. "Yes, Padre. Sorry for my outburst."

Over the years, Valeria and I have learned that the calmer we stay with Alejandro, the quicker and easier our visits can be. My job has been to keep her calm. Her role is to lead the conversation forward so we can get it over with as soon as possible and resume our normal lives.

"As my only legitimate child," he continues, pointing to her, "you should have the right to take over my fortune."

Take over his fortune?

"But only if your husband is running the operation."

I gape at him and remind myself to close my mouth. *Run the operation? Oh, hell no.*

"Alejandro, that's very kind of you to offer, but I have my own business to run and know nothing about yours."

"Yes, I can see that. You've done well with the little resources you had to create your fortune. You have the smarts to expand my operation."

It's the first compliment the man has ever paid me, and my gut is flipping with nausea. *Expand his operation? No, no, no!*

"Padre, Jamison and I want no part of your business. We have our own life in America. I told you, we are never moving to Colombia."

"Yes, well, I've decided it would be smart to have operations run from America instead of Colombia. He can fly back and forth."

I gulp. My mouth goes dry. "Alejandro, that is a very nice offer, but I'm going to pass."

He slams his hands on the table. "You pass on my fortune. My daughter's legal inheritance?"

Oh shit.

"Padre, I do not want nor need your inheritance. Jamison is not one of your men. He is not cut from that cloth. You do not need to involve us in this. Santiago has been your right hand for years. He is qualified to take over and wants to. Let him."

Alejandro's face contorts. His voice lowers. "It is not his legitimate right. It is your legitimate right. I promised your mother I would never take that from you."

He actually made a promise to the woman he wants to keep. That's surprising.

"I will talk to Mama, then. We are not taking over the business," Valeria adamantly states, her face red with anger.

"What I built is not good enough for you? All the years I paid for you to go to school here and your expenses? It was good enough then but not now?"

"No offense, sir, but Valeria was a child. We haven't taken any money since we got married."

He slams his hand down on the table again. "Yes. I know that. That is why I've determined that you are capable of taking over."

I take a deep breath. "Sir—"

"Don't you sir me. My daughter deserves her inheritance, and she will not get it without her husband in charge. You married her, and if you hadn't, she would have married a man who would have been working in my business all these years with me. It's time you stepped into your role."

No. This is not happening.

"I am not stepping into any role. I have my own business to take care of. I'm sorry, Alejandro, but it isn't going to happen," I tell him firmly. I've never spoken to him before in this tone, but enough is enough. I will not get involved in whatever it is he is involved in.

"You will deny my daughter her inheritance?"

"Padre, we don't need any money. We have plenty." Valeria puts her hand on his, trying to calm him.

He looks at their hands then her. "My money isn't good enough for you?"

"It isn't about that."

"You will have nothing from me. What do you do when you go through all your money someday?"

I sigh. "Alejandro, it's a very nice offer, and I appreciate your confidence in my abilities, but Valeria and I have enough money to last a lifetime. Your men who have been with you throughout the years are much better equipped to develop your business. I will continue to take care of Valeria. You have my word on that. She will never go without. But I am not taking over your business."

I've never discussed our financial situation with Alejandro before, and I don't know how much the man has, but I may have more. And mine is all legitimately earned, and in bank accounts, besides a few million I keep in cash in my safe. Valeria also has earned a great deal of money, and I've invested it for her with Noah's companies, so she should never have to worry about anything, either.

He turns to Valeria. "What about your mama? If Santiago takes over, he will push her out. The only home she has known will no longer be hers."

Valeria blinks back tears. "You would let him do that?"

"Once I'm gone, it is his to make decisions on. They have never gotten along. I know my son and what he will do."

"Then, I'll take care of Mama."

He snorts. "A woman does not take care of a woman."

I press my hand on Valeria so she doesn't speak. "I will take care of her, then."

"You've done well, but you don't have my kind of resources."

You don't know shit, asshole. But I'm not going to delve into it more with Alejandro.

"We have enough to take care of her, don't we?" I turn to Valeria.

She knows what we are worth, and she also knows I don't want her father to know. The less he knows about us, the better.

"Yes, we do," Valeria confidently states.

He laughs. "You two are fools."

Valeria stands up. "We are done with this conversation."

"Sit down." Her father points. "You're done when I say you are."

Defiantly, she lifts her chin. "No. We're done here. I'm not under your control anymore."

His eyes slit farther, and he says nothing.

"As you like to remind everyone, a woman's husband is in control." She turns to me. "Jamison, are we done here?"

Fuck. This isn't good. The last thing I want to do is piss Alejandro off.

I stand up and grab her hand. "Alejandro, it's been nice seeing you. Have a safe trip back to Colombia. I will not be taking over your business, and you have my word that I will take care of Valeria's mama." I look at Valeria. "Let's go."

I move to lead Valeria out of the room, but the guard steps in front of the door. "Señor Sánchez has not given you permission to leave."

I pull Valeria in closer to me. "I am her husband. I say when we leave."

"Señor Sánchez says when it's time to leave."

"Let them go. We will resume this conversation another time," Alejandro says from behind us.

I stare the guard in the face. "Move."

He steps aside, and Valeria and I say nothing until we are safe in the car.

"Jamison, I'm so sorry. I didn't know—"

"Don't apologize. I know you didn't have any idea that was coming."

"I never even considered he would think something like that. Santiago has been his right hand for as long as I can remember. He has groomed him to take over. I don't know where this is coming from."

"Whatever he has up his sleeve, I don't want any part of it."

"Nor do I," Valeria assures me.

I turn into her more. "We have plenty of money to take care of your mama. Don't let him influence you regarding her welfare."

"I know that. You don't have to worry about me thinking twice about this. I would never ask you to do this, nor do I want any part of it. You know my father is involved in dangerous activities. I don't want you wrapped up in that."

"I just wanted to reassure you. I can't believe he would allow your mama to be kicked out."

"It's my father. He's heartless."

I chuckle. "Sorry, forgot who we were talking about."

Valeria puts her hand on my leg. "Jamison, we've never defied him before. He isn't going to just let this go."

I sigh. "What can he do? Honestly? He can't make me run his business."

She furrows her brows. "I don't know, but if there is a way to do that, he will find it."

My gut sinks, knowing that everything she says is true. Alejandro is capable of the impossible.

16

Quinn

"I'T'S INCREDIBLE," KIM TELLS ME.

"Really?"

"Yes. The beta readers are raving about your book. Have you not looked?"

"I've been too scared."

"Quinn, logon. Look at what they are saying. Your stories are legit."

My stories are legit.

Don't get too excited, Quinn.

"Okay. I'll log in and read the comments."

"I think you should set up a publishing schedule so you can keep moving forward."

Part of me is excited, and part of me is cringing. This is all still scary for me.

"Let me read the comments first. Can we talk after I've read them?"

"Sure. Read them today though. You need to get your work out into the world."

Excitement bubbles again, even though I try to tell myself to stay levelheaded about this.

I've done a ton of research over the last few months and thrown myself into learning everything involved in self-publishing. I haven't told anyone, including Jamison. I know he wants me to publish, but I don't want to let him down if I decide not to. Kim is the only person who knows, and she convinced me to send my manuscript to the beta readers to see what their feedback was.

In the last few months, Jamison and I have secretly flown back and forth to be with each other. He keeps asking me to move to New York, and I've thought about it a lot, trying to come to terms with moving across the country and having him support me.

Admittedly, I do want to focus on my writing, and the closer I get to publishing, the more open I am to the idea.

I hate my job even more. My boss seems to have gotten meaner, and I hate management. The only good thing about it is that I'm making more money, so I've been able to put some aside. If I do decide to move to New York, at least I will have a small nest egg, so I don't have to completely depend on Jamison until I start to make money from my novels.

I've also looked for editing jobs in New York and submitted my resume to several publishers, but I'm not getting anywhere with that.

As soon as I get off the phone with Kim, Jamison calls.

"Hey," I answer.

"Hey, doll. I just booked to come to Chicago next weekend. I'll email you my flight confirmation."

"Great."

"I wish you would come out this weekend."

"I know, me, too. But I need to figure out this situation at work. Half Dick has been all over me this week."

"Quinn, why are you still putting up with this?"

"We've been over this. It's my job."

"I don't understand why you're fighting me on moving here. It's like you prefer to spend the majority of your week doing something you hate."

I get defensive. "I'm not fighting you. And you know that isn't true."

"Then, move. I've given you plenty of time to get used to the idea. Why can't you choose us?"

"This isn't about choosing us."

"Really? It sure seems that way."

"Have you had a bad day or something?"

The phone goes silent.

"Are you still there?"

"Yes. I'm sorry. I miss you. I hate being away from you. I want you with me. I feel like we're in limbo, waiting for our life to start."

My heart aches. What he's saying I feel, too. I don't know why I can't take this plunge when I love him and want to be with him.

"Jamison, I love you. I'm figuring this out. Please, just give me more time to work on this."

"Okay, doll. I'm sorry for pressuring you, but it's killing me being away from you all the time. If I could move to Chicago, I would, but I can't with the business right now."

"I know. It's killing me, too. I'll figure this out, I promise."

"I have to go, Quinn. My meeting is about to start."

"All right. I love you," I tell him.

"I love you, too. Bye." He hangs up.

I sit back against the couch in shock. Jamison has never gotten angry with me about not moving to New York before. He's been patient over the last few months.

Why am I fighting him on this?

I'm lost in thought, overanalyzing things once more, when my boss fires off four nasty text messages to me, back-to-back, before I can even respond to one of them.

Maybe I am a sucker for punishment. Why am I continuing to stay in this situation when I could have everything I've ever wanted with Jamison?

"He hasn't put a ring on your finger," my mother's voice says in my head.

Ugh. Shut up, Mom.

I open my laptop and log into the Internet site where the beta readers I submitted my book to left their feedback. For the next hour, I'm engrossed in their reviews of my book.

There aren't any bad comments. They are all raving about my story. One reader after another sends me private messages on how impressed they are with my work.

Another two nasty texts come across my phone from my boss, just as one comes in from Jamison.

"I'm sorry, doll. Forgive me for being an ass. I love you," Jamison writes.

What am I doing? He's right. I need to choose us.

Grabbing my laptop again, I search for the next flight out of Chicago to New York.

Two hours. I can make that.

I book the ticket, pack a bag, and head out to the airport. It's only Wednesday, but I'll surprise him. *I have full access to his penthouse. I might as well use it.*

———

FOR THE FIRST TIME IN MY ENTIRE LIFE, I'M IGNORING EVERYTHING my mother or brother has tried to instill in me. I'm trusting in what I know to be true between Jamison and me.

I don't need to stay in a job I hate.

I can let him support me. That's what people in love do, right? They support each other?

Just because my father never committed to my mother and continues to support and buy her with money doesn't mean that Jamison supporting me financially is the same.

No. What we have is different. It's real. We're both committed to each other—only each other.

By the time I get to New York, it's late. I freshen up in the bath-room, hail a cab, and am soon waiving to Conroy, the guard at the front desk in Jamison's lobby.

I push my thumb on the screener, walk through the gate, and hit the code inside the elevator.

The door opens to the penthouse, and I wheel my suitcase out. At first, I think I'm alone, or maybe Jamison is sleeping, but then I hear their voices from the kitchen area.

"Your father has crossed the line, V."

"I know, darling. I'm sorry."

Darling? Why is she calling my boyfriend darling?

"Why can't he understand that you don't need your inheritance. I will take care of you and your mama. Why can't he trust my word on this?" Jamison says.

He'll take care of her and her mama?

"Do you think we should show him our bank statements? Maybe that would stop this madness?" the woman with a slight accent says.

Our bank statements?

"No. I do not want your father having any information on our assets," Jamison sternly says. "Who knows what he would do with that information."

Our assets?

"I'm so sorry. This is so screwed up. Santiago has always been groomed to take over his business. It's never been in the plans for anyone I married to take over, and especially not a non-Colom-bian like you. None of this makes sense."

Anyone I married...like you? Jamison's married? My heart drops, and I turn to leave, but my suitcase turns on its side and falls.

"Quinn!" I hear Jamison say.

Oh God. I have to get out of here. Every single word my mother or brother has ever said to me screams out in my head.

How big a fool have I been? How could he do this to me?

I push the button to the elevator. *Open. Oh God, please open.*

"Quinn." Jamison spins me around.

Tears are streaming down my face. "You're married."

"It's not what you think."

I slap him as hard as I can.

He slowly turns his face back to me. My handprint is on his cheek. "I deserve that for not telling you, but it's not what you think."

I turn back to the elevator. *Why isn't it opening?*

Jamison grabs my arm. "Quinn, come sit down. Let's talk so I can explain."

I spin into him. "Explain? Explain what? That you've lied to me all these months. Does your wife know about me?"

"Yes. And it's not what you think," Jamison repeats.

"Please, Quinn. Let him explain." The woman comes out of the kitchen, and my mouth hangs open. It's Valeria Sánchez. You can't get groceries without her face staring back at you in the checkout counter.

I point between them. "You two are married?"

"Not how you think," Jamison says.

"It's true."

I hurl at him, "I don't understand. Is there another version of married I don't know about?"

"Yes," they both say at the same time.

"How long have you been married?"

Jamison gulps. "Fifteen years."

"Fifteen years," I cry out. "And you didn't think to tell me?"

"Quinn, come sit down." He tries to put his arm on my shoulder, and I duck out of it.

"Do not touch me."

"Quinn, please, come sit down," Valeria quietly says.

I am confused. "You do realize that I've been sleeping with your husband, correct?"

She gives me a sympathetic smile. "Yes. Please come sit down."

"Quinn, sit down and let us explain," Jamison repeats.

I don't know what to do. I'm so confused.

He's married.

Tears trickle down my face again. "You lied to me."

"I never lied to you."

"You didn't tell me you were married."

"No, but you never asked me if I was, and I never told you I wasn't. I didn't lie to you."

I snarl, "I think the first night we met when I asked you if you had a girlfriend, that would have been the appropriate time to tell me that you have a wife."

He closes his eyes as if in pain. "I'm sorry. But if you let me explain, you'll understand why I couldn't."

"So I would sleep with you," I seethe as more tears run down my face.

"No. Sit down. Let me explain. Please." He tries to grab my arm again.

"Stop trying to touch me," I yell.

He holds his hands up. "Okay. Please sit down."

"Quinn, I understand you're upset, but please come sit down so we can explain," Valeria calmly says.

"Why are you not upset? You should be upset," I tell her.

She steps forward and grabs my hand. "Come on. Come sit with me." For some reason, unbeknownst to me, I allow her to lead me to the sofa.

What is going on here? Why is she being kind to me? I've been sleeping with her husband.

I sit, and she sits next to me. She continues to hold my hand. Her body is turned into mine, and her one leg is bent, with her knee on the back of the couch.

"What we are about to tell you cannot go further than this room," she says.

I say nothing.

"Jamison and I are married, but we did not marry for love."

"I don't understand."

"I'm sure. My girlfriend Cindy didn't understand when I told her, either."

Her girlfriend? What? I'm so confused.

"Jamison and I have always been good friends. I am a lesbian. We've only kissed twice. Once at each of our weddings."

More hurt courses through me. "You got married not once but twice?"

He takes a deep breath. "Yes, and we will tell you why, doll."

"Do not call me doll. I am not your doll," I angrily fire at him.

He gives me another pained look. "Don't say that."

Disgust fills me.

Valeria says, "He married me when we were twenty, so I could stay in the United States and not have to marry one of my father's men back in Colombia. We went to the courthouse. My father found out and made us have a big wedding in Colombia. Jamison only did it to save me from a life I could not bear to live."

What? Is this a big act?

"I understand this is shocking. My father is a very dangerous man. He is involved in the criminal world. I did not know when Jamison married me what my father was involved in. I was fourteen when I came to the United States for school and never left. When we got married, my father visited us and set the rules down."

"The rules?"

"Yes. The rules."

Jamison comes and sits on the ottoman in front of me. "The rules were that we either got an immediate annulment, and Valeria went back to Colombia and married one of her father's men, or we got married what he considered the right way."

"The right way?"

He nods.

Valeria cuts in. "My father takes marriage seriously. He cheats on my mother and has seven illegitimate children, but he views marriage as a lifelong commitment." Her voice is full of disgust.

Lifelong commitment. Jamison is in a lifelong commitment to Valeria Sánchez, his wife.

Her father has illegitimate children...like me.

My hand flies to my face as I swallow the bile that crawls up my esophagus.

Jamison quickly moves onto the couch next to me and pulls me into his chest as more tears fall down my face. "It's just a piece of paper for Valeria and me. She loves Cindy, and I love you. This doesn't change anything."

I push out of his grasp. "This doesn't change anything? How can you say that? Were you even going to tell me?"

He looks at Valeria. "V, can we have a minute?"

"Sure." She pats my hand and leaves the room.

"As soon as you told me you would move to New York, I was going to tell you."

"What does that have to do with it?"

"I wanted to make sure you were committed to me...to us."

"Committed to you? I've never cheated on anyone—"

"That's not what I mean, Quinn. This doesn't just involve me. I've never told anyone I've dated this before. I was going to tell you, but I wanted to be positive you were sure about me first."

"Sure about you? I've been trying to figure out all the things I needed to move here. It's all I've thought about. *You're* all I've thought about."

"I screwed up. I'm sorry. I never would intentionally hurt you."

"I came here to tell you I would move."

He cups my face. "Good. Nothing has changed."

Tears fall down my cheeks. "Everything has changed."

His green eyes intensely stare into mine. "No, it hasn't. Nothing has changed."

"How can you say that?" I choke out.

"You are the only person I have ever loved. Nothing has changed. I told you why I'm married. I'm sorry I didn't tell you sooner, and you found out this way. But nothing has changed."

"For you. Nothing has changed for you, Jamison."

He closes his eyes then opens them. "I know this isn't normal, and it's a shock, but why does this have to change anything for you?"

I'll always be the mistress.

"You know why."

He sternly says, "This is not the same thing as your parents."

"Isn't it?"

"No. It's not even close."

I look away from him.

His voice gets quieter. "Are you telling me you no longer love me?"

My head jerks toward him. "Of course not."

"Then nothing has changed. I still want to spend my life with you. Move here. Everything we talked about can still be. Let me love you and take care of you."

"Love me and take care of me as your mistress?" More tears fall.

"Quinn, stop—"

"No. I can't think right now. I need to go." I jump off the couch.

Jamison stands in front of me. "It's after midnight. You aren't going anywhere."

"I'll get a hotel room."

He puts his arms on my shoulders. "Please stop. Stay in my room. I'll stay out, and we can talk tomorrow. You can't leave like this, and not at this hour."

I look away from him.

He pulls me into his arms. "Quinn, please. It's late."

I start to cry harder.

His arms wrap tighter around me. "I'm sorry. So sorry. I should have told you sooner. I've only ever loved you. I want to spend my life with you. Nothing has changed."

I can't stop crying, and I should push out of his hold on me, but I can't.

"Shh," he whispers against my head while stroking my hair. "I love you so much. I only want to be with you."

And that's what hurts the most. He isn't only with me.

17

Jamison

I MISJUDGED OUR SITUATION. NOT TELLING QUINN ABOUT VALERIA and me was the biggest mistake I could have made.

Quinn's in my arms, crying. I've hurt her—not surface-level hurt but deep hurt. And it's breaking my heart.

"Shh. I'm so sorry," I tell her again, wishing I could get a do-over.

She cries for several minutes and begins to calm down.

"Let me grab your bag and let's go to my room. You can't leave tonight. It's too late."

Her eyes painfully shut, and she slowly nods.

I kiss the top of her head and grab her bag. When I turn and come around the corner, she's already gone to my room.

When I get there, she's staring out the window, with one arm across her chest and one hand over her face. I set the bag by the wall and shut the door.

How could I have been so stupid?

I cross the room to her. Fresh tears are streaming down her cheeks. I stand behind her and wrap my arms around her waist. Putting my cheek next to hers, I say, "Tell me what I can do to make this right."

"Get a divorce," she whispers.

I sigh. "I would. But I can't. Tell me anything else."

The river of tears runs faster. "Why not?

"V will get hurt. I probably would, too."

"I don't understand."

I turn her to me. "Quinn, V's father is not to be messed with. If he finds out we lied to him all these years, he will probably cut my eyes out before he kills me. His men will track V down and take her back to Colombia, where who knows what will happen to her."

"But she's his daughter. Surely he wouldn't hurt her?"

"He will hurt anyone who defies him. We lied. We defied him. He wanted her married to one of his men. We stopped that. She's a lesbian. There will be consequences."

"So, you're going to just stay married for the rest of your life?"

I cup her face in my hands. "Neither V nor I want to stay married. V and her girlfriend Cindy wish to get married, too. We've looked at every angle. There is no way to get out of this without both of us getting hurt. These are dangerous people."

Quinn furrows her brows and licks her lips. "So you and me, we would never be able to get married. I would always be your mistress."

I close my eyes. "Stop saying you're my mistress. You aren't."

"I am. Your wife is not me. You screw me. That makes me your mistress."

"Stop. You're no such thing."

"I would marry you right now if I could. But it's just a piece of paper."

"It's not to me."

I sigh. "We could have a wedding, exchange vows, do everything except make it legal. It doesn't define how I feel about you or what you mean to me."

My heart bleeds further as more tears drip out of her eyes.

"I was twenty years old. It was supposed to be for three, four years tops. I thought I was helping a friend. Neither V nor I knew the consequences."

Minutes pass. Quinn finally says, "I don't understand how you kept this from the press. How do they not know Valeria Sánchez is married?"

"She used her mother's maiden name. Gómez is her real last name and on our marriage certificate."

She closes her eyes as if pained at the notion of a marriage certificate.

I pull her over to the bed. "Put your pajamas on, get in bed, and I'll tell you whatever you want to know."

She takes a shaky breath but nods. "Okay."

I grab her suitcase, open it up on the bed, find her nightshirt, and hand it to her. "Let me go throw a pair of shorts on."

"Okay."

I quickly change, and when I get back, she has changed but is standing by the window again.

"Quinn, come to bed." I put my arm around her waist and lead her to the bed, pull the covers back, and she slides in.

I slip under the covers next to her and pull her into my arms.

"Who knows you're married?"

"My parents and siblings. Chase, Noah, Xander, and Cindy. That's it. Oh, and Mary, who is V's best friend. She was her roommate fifteen years ago. She's the one who suggested we get married so V didn't get deported. Xander's ex-girlfriend Billie...but she doesn't know the real story. And our old friend Matt, who we don't talk to anymore because he slept with Chase's girlfriend."

She gapes. "Your friend did what?"

"Let's talk about that another time."

"Okay, but Chase knew and didn't say anything to me?"

I sigh. "Quinn, I've never told anyone before you."

"You only told me because I walked into your conversation."

"That's not true. I was going to tell you when you told me you would move. I'm not lying. Ask V."

"I don't want to ask your wife," she snaps.

I don't say anything.

"I'm sorry. I don't mean to be nasty about her. She seems nice."

"I told her the day after I first asked you to move in that I was in love with you and wanted you to move to New York. She told me to tell you about our situation. I should have listened to her. I'm sorry."

"So you assumed this entire time that I wasn't fully committed to you just because I was figuring out how to make this big move?"

I kiss the top of her head. "I thought maybe you weren't sure about us."

"How could you think that?"

I sigh. "I don't understand what is keeping you in Chicago when we can be together."

"I told you what my reasons were."

"I know you did. But it doesn't make sense to me."

"Why is it so hard for you to understand?"

"Quinn."

She rolls onto her side so she's facing me. "No. What is so hard about it?"

"Do you really want to get into this right now?"

"Now seems as good a time as any."

"Okay. I have money. More than enough so neither of us would ever have to work again. There is no logical reason why you haven't moved here unless you have questions about us."

She sits up.

Oh great.

"No logical reason? I'm supposed to move halfway across the country without even thinking about it? I'm supposed to stop working—"

"No! I said you could work on your writing career. Or find another job here if that's what you really want."

She snorts. "Do you know how many resumes I've sent out here?"

"You sent resumes out?"

"Yes, Jamison. I have. Do you know how many?"

"No."

"Ten. Every week, I've sent my resume to ten different places. Some I've sent multiple times. Do you know how many have given me an interview?"

Why didn't she tell me? I quietly say, "No."

"Zero. Do you know what it's like to get rejected every week, over and over, and continue to keep doing the same thing?"

"Shit. Quinn, I didn't know. Why didn't you tell me?"

"That's an awesome conversation piece. 'Hey, babe, I had another ten companies reject me this week.' Sorry if I didn't want to discuss it."

I scrub my face with my hands. "I didn't know. I wish you'd told me."

"In the meantime, I've been researching everything there is to know about self-publishing and even had my book sent to beta readers. Kim's been helping me. And I've been saving my money from the raise I got so when I move I have some sort of nest egg, so I hopefully don't have to spend all your money while I'm getting my author career started or finding my next job."

"You sent your book out?"

"Yes."

"I'm proud of you. Why didn't you tell me?"

"Because you want it so badly, I don't want to disappoint you if it fails," she cries out.

I pull her into me. "Quinn, you aren't going to fail."

"You don't know that."

"I do."

"You don't."

I put my face next to hers. "Listen to me. You will never disappoint me. No matter what happens, I'm proud of you, but you aren't going to fail. You have real talent."

"Talent doesn't mean anything."

"It does. And you don't need to save money to come here. I told you I would take care of you."

She bites her lip, shakes her head, and stares at me.

"What?"

"You don't get it."

"What don't I get?"

"It's not easy for me to let go of my independence."

"I'm not asking you to."

"If you bankroll me, I have no independence."

"I told you I would give you a card. I'll give you an unlimited spending limit. You can have the code to my safe so you can grab cash if you want."

She grabs my face. "That doesn't give me independence."

I close my eyes. "Quinn, you aren't making any sense to me."

"Earning money gives me independence. Taking yours doesn't."

"I disagree."

"Okay. You're allowed to disagree, but you aren't the one being asked to change your entire life."

"I told you I can't move to Chicago right now because of work. I own a company. It makes more sense for you to move here."

"I know. And I finally was okay with it all tonight. It all came together for me. I wanted to tell you that I was ready to move and let you take care of me."

"Good. I'll call the moving company." I pull her into me to kiss her.

"No." She leans away from my lips. "I can't move here."

"Quinn—"

"No, Jamison. You didn't trust me enough to tell me you were married. You expected me to change my entire life for you, but you didn't trust me."

This mistake I made fifteen years ago just continues to spread.

My heart races. "I do trust you. I made a bad judgment call about when to tell you. But I've never lied or been unfaithful. I always planned on telling you. Don't give up on me because I made a mistake."

Her voice gets softer. "I'm not giving up on you. I love you. But I can't move here."

My mouth goes dry. "Quinn, don't do this. Nothing has changed."

She quietly says, "You need to stop saying that because everything has changed."

18

Quinn

"ARE YOU BREAKING UP WITH ME?" JAMISON'S BLINKING BACK tears, and so am I.

"No. Yes. I don't know." I throw my hands in the air, frustrated.

He cups my face. "Please. Give me another chance. I know I messed up. I love you."

A tear escapes my eye. "I love you."

"Then we can get past this."

"Can we?"

"Yes."

I look away as the dam breaks once more.

He pulls me into him and kisses my tears. "I want to spend my life with you. We're meant to be together."

"You're married," I whisper as the hurt of the evening comes crashing back to me.

"I told you, so did V, it's just a piece of paper. It doesn't mean anything."

But it does. It means you'll never fully be mine.

He wraps me in his arms, tight, and I sink into him, not wanting him to let me go but not sure what to even make of all this.

The truth of their marriage makes everything gray. If he were in a typical marriage, I would have already run. But he married Valeria to save her from an awful life, and I can't hate him for it. I wish I could, but I can't.

And she seems nice. I like her. I want to hate her, but I can't. I want to hate him, but that's impossible.

So everything is gray, and I don't know what to do.

My advice to Piper about Noah is ringing in my ears. "Piper, life isn't two plus two equals four. You have to step into the gray area at some point."

But can I turn an eye on this? *Regardless of the circumstances, he's married and didn't tell me.*

His lips move across my jaw, and I can't resist him. He presses his mouth hard against mine as his hand pushes my head into him further while rolling his tongue urgently on mine.

And I'm falling. I'm falling into everything that is Jamison and me. The perfection of our lips, tongue, and breath. The melting of our skin against the other's. The gliding, digging, and grasping of our hands.

"I love you," he murmurs in my mouth. "Nothing has changed."

"Everything has," I repeat, as I lock my hands around his head.

"No, it hasn't." He moves his hand to the strap of my nightgown and lowers it down my arm so my breast is exposed to him. He dips his head down and gently licks around my areola, teasing and taunting my nipple so it puckers.

As he lowers my other strap and plays with my other breast, my legs automatically widen. I wrap my feet over his calves, bucking my lower body against his erection.

I kiss his forehead, and his mouth crushes against mine once more. His fingers slide through my hair, and he pulls my head back as his lips brush my neck.

"You're mine. I'm yours," he mumbles near my ear.

More than anything, I want to be his and him to be mine. It's all I've wanted since I first laid eyes on him from afar.

But how can he be mine when he's married? He's technically hers.

But they've never had a physical relationship. They've only kissed twice, at each of their weddings.

Two weddings. Two sets of vows. Two "I do's."

He rocks his hips on me, grinding his hard erection into my aching sex that's already throbbing for him. His hands lower, wadding up my nightgown and removing it then my panties.

Holding my leg in the air, he shimmies out of his shorts then kisses my ankle, trailing his mouth up to my calf, through my inner thigh, and positions both my legs over his shoulders.

I'm already breathing hard. Wrapping his hands around my hips, he pulls me closer to his face, and the slow burn of my climatic journey begins. His nimble tongue dives in and out of my body, devouring me. He tortures all my nerves and drives me to the edge, expertly keeping my sex pulsing and me loudly begging for more.

"Jamison...oh..." I cry out.

"I got you, doll," he growls, between flicking and sucking me harder.

"I...don't...oh..." My eyes roll back in my head, and the army of flutters rolls through my belly as my cells all burst into a state of euphoric chaos.

I'm erupting against his mouth, digging my hands into his head as he yanks my body hard into his lips.

"Oh God!" I yell as I start to move into another orgasm before my first one has even ended.

The tidal waves of adrenaline hit me, crashing and rolling with speed. When he releases me, he quickly grabs a condom, rolls it on, and enters me before I've caught my breath.

"Oh...oh..." I breathe as my body encloses his length and girth.

"I love you, Quinn. Nothing has changed," he murmurs as my orgasm enters my mouth from his tongue.

I wrap my legs around him tightly and thrust my hips up to match his downward movement.

My fingers dig into his back, the heel of my palm pressing into him forcefully.

He circles his cock, swiping hard, hitting my sweet spot, stretching my walls.

"Jamison," I cry out.

"I love you."

I whimper against him as I spasm, clutching his cock with increasing speed and pressure.

"That's it. I got you, doll."

I can't focus my eyes. I pant and see whiteness and stars. A loud moan escapes me as I burst once again into the paradise of pleasure that no one except Jamison has ever given me.

"Nothing has changed," he repeats, as he thrusts into me harder and faster, hitting my G-spot and sending me into multiple peaks of endorphins.

I don't even know what I'm yelling out anymore. My body is like a pinball, pinging back and forth between one high to the next as Jamison tightens his embrace.

When he finally pumps hard, I convulse, and my toes curl from the bolt of fire surging up my legs and throughout me.

He collapses on me as our orgasms collide, and we bury our faces in each other's necks.

My heart beats so hard against my chest cavity, I think it might pop. Sweat rolls off us.

Jamison smashes his lips to mine, kissing me as if there is no tomorrow, no other opportunity, no additional chance, and this is it. He puts his all into it, worshipping me, trying to claim me, on a mission to show me nothing has changed, and we are still meant to be together.

"Tell me you still love me, doll," he says between kisses.

I don't hesitate. It's the truth. "I still love you, Jamison."

He pushes his forehead to mine. "Tell me you haven't given up on me and we can figure this out."

I stare into his green eyes full of fear and love. "I haven't given up on you, and we can figure this out," I quietly say.

"Good. Whatever I need to do to make this up to you, I will."

How will you do that if you can't get divorced?

19

Quinn

IGNORANCE IS BLISS. WHOEVER SAID THAT WAS SMART. THEY MUST
have known heartache.

And heartache is all I feel.

All month, I've had limited contact with Jamison. I told him I
needed some time to process everything.

"Nothing has changed. You're the only woman I've ever loved,
and I want to spend my life with you. Whatever I need to do so
you're comfortable moving here, and to make up for this, I will.
We're meant to be together, doll." He kissed me like I was his
entire world. We were at the airport, and I blinked back tears as I
left him behind.

When I got through security, I got a text. "I love you."

I went into the bathroom stall and broke down sobbing.

Jamison keeps asking to come to Chicago or for me to come to New York for the weekend, but I keep making excuses. He keeps sending me flowers every day, but instead of the happiness they used to bring me, I now feel sadness with each new delivery.

It's a reminder of how everything felt so right with him, yet so much is so wrong.

The month away from him has done nothing for my heart. Every day I'm not with him, the ache deepens.

I've thrown myself into my writing to pass the time and not run after him. But also to give me something besides thinking about how this could work between us, knowing he's married.

Jamison and Valeria told me all the details. The day after I learned the truth, I talked further with Valeria, and she even gave me Cindy's number. She told me that if anyone understood what I was going through, it would be Cindy and that she was waiting for my call. She also told me that she waited two years to tell Cindy about Jamison.

Logically, I know I should call Cindy if only to talk to someone about what is going on, but I don't. So I suffer in silence all day, thinking about whether Jamison and I can really have a life together now or not. And I try all day not to cry anytime I think about not having him in my life.

Nighttime is the worst. I not only cry myself to sleep, but my mother's and brother's voices are in my head. And I can't hide from them.

I am a mistress.

"Stop saying that. You are not my mistress," Jamison adamantly says whenever I bring it up.

"I'm the textbook definition of one," I always reply.

"Quinn, why can't you let this go? I'm not a husband cheating on his wife. You know the situation. We can have the same fabulous life together we were going to before you found out."

"What does that make me, then?"

"The woman I love. My heart and soul. The one I choose to spend my life with and take care of."

I never respond. I don't know what to say to that, and I always end up in tears.

My phone buzzes, yanking me out of my thoughts.

"Doll, I'm in town for work. Can I take you to lunch, please?" Jamison writes.

My heart rate increases. *He's in Chicago?*

"Why didn't you tell me you were coming?"

"Sorry. You used to like it when I surprised you."

Stop being nasty. He's right. It's something I love about him.

"I'm sorry. That didn't sound very nice. Where do you want to meet?"

"I'll pick you up."

"Let's just meet. I'm not in the office right now," I lie to him.

Do not get in a car with him. Being out in public is safe. Stay in the safe zone.

"I can swing by wherever you are."

"It's okay. Just tell me where to meet you."

A minute passes, and I finally receive a text. "Kincaid's. Do you know where it is?"

Yep, but I've only been there with my brother, who hates me right now.

I still haven't spoken to my brother since our most recent nasty text exchange. The last thing I want to do is run into him, especially when Jamison and I are trying to figure out where we stand.

I grab a cab over to Kincaid's. My insides are shaking, and I remind myself it's just lunch. We're in public. Nothing can happen, and it's safe.

Jamison is waiting for me. As soon as I set foot inside the building, he quickly pulls me into his arms, and I sink into his warmth. The familiar warmth of his body, the clean, woody scent of his skin, and the way his arms wrap around me, I've missed more than I could comprehend. Tears come to my eyes, and I smash my face against his suit jacket.

"Hey," he softly says, stroking my head. "I've missed you so much." He kisses the top of my head, and tears start to fall out of my eyes.

"Doll, what's wrong?" he gently asks.

I pull back and wipe my eyes. "Nothing."

"Quinn?" He cups my face.

I bite my lip and stare into his beautiful green eyes that I've missed.

"This is so hard," I whisper.

"It's killing me."

"I feel like my heart is being ripped out of my chest."

His eyes fill with tears. "Nothing has changed. I love you. Tell me what I need to do so we can get past this. Please. I'll do anything."

"I don't know."

Pain crosses his face. "I don't think staying away from each other is the solution. Do you think this is helping us move forward?"

Is it helping?

"No," I admit quietly.

He weaves his fingers through my hair and tilts my head up before gently brushing his lips on mine. "Then let's stop staying away from each other. Can we agree on that?"

I don't even think. "Yes."

"Good. Come back to New York with me."

"I can't. I have too much going on at work. Can you stay?"

He sighs. "I have to be back tonight. I have a meeting at six a.m. tomorrow with one of the hospitals."

"Okay."

"What about this weekend? I have a board meeting and charity events over the weekend. You could come with me to the events."

"It's my mom's birthday. I have a family dinner to attend."

"Have you talked to your brother yet?"

"No."

"Are you going to before you see him?"

"I don't know."

He wraps me into his arms, making me feel safe and loved as if no one but us exists. "How long is your lunch break?"

"An hour, but I can get away with ninety minutes."

He kisses the top of my head. "Okay, doll. Let's go eat."

We walk into the restaurant and quickly are seated in a quiet booth. Jamison slides next to me and puts his arm around my shoulder.

All the lonely nights and emotion-filled days of thinking about him and trying to figure everything out without him suddenly seem like the wrong way to figure this out.

I need to figure it out with him.

"I wish you didn't have to go," I blurt out.

"I'll be back next weekend. Chase and I have some things to do for work in Chicago, but I think Noah is getting a VIP room at Club D for Friday night. Unless you're ready to tell everyone about us, I don't see how we are getting out of Club D."

Am I ready to tell everyone about us? No. What are you going to say when they ask questions about your relationship, and you don't even know the answers?

"I'm not ready. We have things we need to figure out."

"All right. We can keep it as it is. But can I take you out Saturday so we can spend some time on our own?"

"Yes."

"At least we can dance together all night." He wiggles his eyebrows.

The waitress comes and takes our order and leaves.

Jamison's phone rings. He cringes. "I'm sorry, doll, but I have to take this."

"It's okay. Go ahead."

"V, I just sat down for lunch with Quinn, and her time is limited. Can I call you back?"

He brushes the back of his fingers on my cheek, but it doesn't do anything to calm my shaking insides.

Of course he has to take his phone call. It's his wife.

Stop it, Quinn. Valeria is kind and wants you with Jamison. It must be important.

She will always be his number one priority. They exchanged vows.

"He did what?" Jamison shakes his head.

I put my hand on his leg.

"Okay, V. I'll call you later. We need to figure this out." He hangs up.

"Jamison, what's wrong?"

He looks up at the ceiling then in my eyes. "Nothing to worry about doll. Just more ways V's father is stepping over the line."

The hairs on my neck stand up. "What do you mean? Are you in danger?"

"No. Everything is fine."

"Tell me what is going on?"

"It's better if you don't know."

More secrets. So your wife can know, but I can't?

"Of course, stupid girl, you're the mistress," I hear my mother's voice say.

I look away.

"Hey," Jamison says sternly. "This is for your safety. You have to trust me on this."

"Trust you?"

"Yes. Trust me."

"Jamison?" a familiar voice says.

"You've gotta be kidding me," my brother's voice rings in my ears.

My gut drops.

Jamison turns, and I look up. Steven, and his friend Matt, who I dated for two months and was the last guy I slept with before Jamison, are standing in front of our table. Matt works with my brother, and Steven kept telling me to go out with him. I was fresh out of a long-term relationship and feeling lonely, so I did. The only person I regret sleeping with is him. My brother was not happy when I broke up with Matt.

"Matt. What are you doing here?" Jamison clenches his jaw.

"I live here. What are you doing here?" Matt asks.

My brother glares at us as Jamison doesn't flinch. "I'm having lunch with my girlfriend. Steven, how are you?"

My brother takes a deep breath.

"You and Quinn are together?" Matt asks.

"Yes, we are. Do you two know each other?" Jamison looks at me, and I cringe.

"Yes. How do you two know each other?" I point between Jamison and Matt.

Jamison shifts in his seat. "Matt used to hang out with Chase, Noah, Xander, and I."

My mouth hangs open. *Matt is the one who slept with Chase's girlfriend?*

"We dated, didn't we, Quinn." Matt gives me a cocky stare.

Heat rushes to my cheeks, and Jamison looks at me then quickly back to Matt and Steven.

My brother points between Jamison and Matt. "You two are friends?"

"Used to be are the keywords," Jamison says.

Matt laughs softly. "Still backing your boy without knowing the full story, huh?"

Jamison glares. "I don't need to know that story."

"I would think that you of all people would understand the value of others knowing the full story before passing judgments. Have you spoken to Valeria lately?"

Jamison's face reddens. "Don't you speak her name."

"Who's Valeria? Why are you getting upset about another woman when my sister is sitting next to you?" My brother speaks up.

"Steven, stay out of this," I cry out.

"Steven, now's not the time," Jamison says.

Matt laughs. "Valeria is Jamison's wife. Or is she your ex-wife now? Did Alejandro finally give you your freedom?"

Jamison jumps out of the booth and grabs Matt by the throat. "You always were a piece of shit. You know that?"

"Jamison," I call out.

My brother steps up to Jamison. "Take your hands off him. You're making a scene."

I glance around and see the other tables have all stopped eating and talking and are watching our interactions.

Jamison lets go of Matt. "Stay out of my business." He looks at my brother. "You and I need to sit down one of these days and talk."

My brother sneers. "Are you married?"

Jamison doesn't answer him.

My brother growls, "I told you to stay away from him, Quinn. You're just as bad as Mom."

"Stop it. You don't know anything," I cry out.

"Get out of this, Quinn. Before it's too late."

"Steven—"

He holds up his hand. "No. There is nothing you can say to justify this." He turns to Jamison. "Stay away from my sister."

"Not going to happen, and you don't know what you're talking about. Get your facts straight first," Jamison sternly says.

"I've got my facts straight, alright. And anything I don't know, it sounds like Matt can fill me in on."

"Yep," Matt says.

The manager comes over with several other male waiters. "Do we need to call the police?"

Everyone shakes their heads.

"We're just leaving," my brother tells him. "Let's go, Matt."

"Nice seeing you, Jamison," Matt throws a final dig. "Quinn." He arrogantly winks at me and follows my brother out of the restaurant.

I put my hands over Jamison's clenched fists. "Sit down."

He joins me. "You dated Matt?"

"Yes. My brother kept bugging me to go out with him."

He looks away.

"Are you upset with me?" I cry out.

"No! I'm sorry, Quinn. I'm sorry about this entire scenario."

I look in his eyes, feeling as if we're at the beginning of the end, and I don't know how to change the course.

20

Jamison

"You all should know, Matt's living in Chicago," I text Chase, Noah, and Xander once I drop Quinn off at work and head to the airport.

"How do you know that?" Noah replies.

"I had a not-so-friendly encounter with him."

"What happened?" Chase asks.

"I can't get into it now. I'll come over and talk to you tonight when I get back," I reply.

"Just going into surgery. I'll call you later, Jamison," Xander texts.

I arrive at the airport, check in, and get through security as boarding begins. Since I'm in business class, I'm one of the first people on the plane, and I settle into my seat, quickly getting lost in thought.

Quinn dated Matt. She slept with him. The thought of him touching her makes my stomach churn. She didn't tell me she slept with him, but I could see it on both their faces.

Matt is friends with Quinn's brother. How he could let that douchebag touch his sister and then stand in the restaurant looking smug is beyond me.

Matt knows V and my history. He went to Colombia and was in the wedding party. He was part of V's and my life for almost eight years. *What is he going to tell Quinn's brother?*

Steven. He has so many notions of me, I don't know if he's ever going to give me a fair shot. And now he knows I'm married and hates me more. *Rightly so.*

I can't say I blame him. If Quinn were my sister, I wouldn't want her with a married guy, either.

But he doesn't know the entire story. I can only imagine how Matt is going to spin this.

My flight is quick, and after it lands I hurry through the airport. My private driver is waiting for me, and I text Chase. "You home?"

"Yeah, come over."

"On my way."

During the drive, I call Quinn.

"Did you get back safely?" she answers instead of saying hello.

"Yeah, doll. Hey, do you want me to fly back this weekend and go to your mom's birthday with you? Then you don't have to fight the firing squad alone?"

"You have things going on in New York—"

"Those aren't as important as you. I can come back and go with you."

She doesn't say anything for a moment. "That's nice of you to offer, but I think it will make things worse right now. My brother already sent me a text message."

"What did it say?"

"It was just a picture of Valeria. I responded that he needs to not be sharing that information and doesn't know the real story."

I close my eyes. That asshole Matt. "Quinn, I haven't seen Matt in eight years, but he's not a good guy."

"I know that," she says quietly.

Something in her voice tells me that she isn't referring to him banging Chase's girlfriend. "What happened?"

"Nothing," she quickly says.

"Quinn, don't tell me nothing."

"Matt was just an asshole when I told him I didn't want to see him anymore. He called me a bunch of names."

"And your brother is still friends with him?"

"I didn't tell my brother. I figured he was just hurt. My brother works with him, and they are friends, so I didn't want to make things awkward for him."

This isn't good. It can't get out that Valeria and I are married. The press would eat us alive. And it can't get out who Valeria's father is. "I'm sorry being with me is causing family issues for you. Are you sure you don't want me to come this weekend?"

"I'm sure. I'll see you next weekend when you come back."

"Okay. I'll call you later. Love you."

"I love you, too." She hangs up.

I text Valeria. "Ran into Matt while in Chicago. Heads up—he's friends with Quinn's brother, who already hates me, and Matt told her brother about us and who you are."

"That slimy weasel."

"Yep."

"Okay. Thanks for the warning."

The car pulls up to Chase's building, and as soon as I walk into the penthouse, he hands me a beer. "What the fuck happened?"

I tell him the story and how Quinn's brother sent her a picture of Valeria.

"I see eight years hasn't made Matt any less of an asshole," Chase seethes.

"Nope."

"God help me if I run into him while I'm in Chicago. I might end up in jail." Chase takes a swig of beer.

"Trust me. It took all I had not to wipe his cocky look off his face. Oh, and he slept with Quinn."

Chase's eyes widen. "What?"

"Her brother pressured her to go out with him. I didn't ask her, but I could tell by the look on both their faces that they slept together. And he was nasty to her when she broke it off."

"Jeez."

I take a long drink of my beer.

"Are you and Quinn okay?"

"I don't know. She agreed to stop staying away from me, but she's still hurt. I'm such an idiot for not telling her sooner."

"You're in a tricky position. Don't beat yourself up too much."

"Easier said than done."

———

THINGS HAVE BEEN STRAINED BETWEEN QUINN AND ME AGAIN. HER mom's birthday ended with her leaving in tears, and I can tell she's pulled back again. I told her I was going to fly in, but she was adamant that I not and told me not to surprise her, either.

So, the last few weeks have been torture. I can't eat or sleep much, constantly worrying about Quinn and wondering what I can do to make everything right between us.

The trip to Chicago doesn't come soon enough. When Chase and I land, we stop to pick up Vivian then Quinn. When the car pulls up to her building, I jump out, ready to kiss her, and remind her that we have something special and that I'm hers, but she's already in the lobby and bolting outside.

She doesn't want me upstairs alone with her.

We hug, but I only get a peck on her cheek. "You look beautiful."

She doesn't say anything, only stares at my eyes, biting her lip.

"I've missed you. No, scratch that. I'm dying without you," I tell her.

She takes a deep breath and closes her eyes painfully. "I'm struggling, too."

My heart races that she's admitted to me that she still cares as deeply about me as I do about her.

Maybe we just need to have a good time, and I can remind her how good we are together.

I brush my thumb along her jawline. "Then let's go have fun tonight, doll. I think we deserve a night of only fun."

She smiles at me. "That sounds like a great idea. I think I need that."

Good. Maybe she will relax a bit and realize that nothing has changed.

"Since it's only Vivian and Chase in the car, can I kiss you properly? We might not get another chance tonight until we're alone."

She looks around then back at me. "Yes."

I lace my fingers through her soft hair, bend down, and put everything I have into showing her I'm still her man, that she's the only woman I've ever loved, that we can still have an amazing life together as planned.

She moans in my mouth, and I groan, lost in the love that she's giving me that I've been craving and aching for over the last few weeks.

When we pull back from the kiss, we're both breathless, and I have her locked in my arms. "That's more like us," I murmur against her lips.

"I've missed you." She blinks tears.

"Shh. I know. I've missed you. Let's enjoy the evening and not think tonight. Let's just be us."

Her glassy blue eyes stare into mine, and it pains me that she's hurting so much—that I've hurt her so much.

I brush my thumbs against her cheeks. "Let me love you tonight, doll. Don't analyze it."

She shuts her eyes and takes a deep breath. "Okay."

I press my lips against hers again.

"We should get in the car," she mumbles.

"All right." I lead her to the car, and we both get in. After she greets Vivian and Chase, I pull her into my chest, and it's like nothing has ever been wrong between us. She's where she should be, with me, and my false sense of security sets in.

We get to Piper and Noah's penthouse and move into friend-zone mode. Quinn and I are still sitting next to each other, but the facade that she puts on in front of anyone besides Vivian and Chase is back.

I wish she would just stop pretending we aren't together.

But this is your fault. She was ready to move to New York, but you didn't tell her when you should have.

I fall into our role and don't touch her, don't call her doll, or reference anything that could be related to one of our private conversations.

Xander and Charlotte surprise us when they show up together, and we eventually all pile into a limo Noah hired for the night and head out to Club D.

After a few drinks, I'm relieved when we leave the VIP room and all hit the dance floor. I don't have to worry about not touching Quinn and take full advantage of the situation.

Quinn and I stay on the dance floor all night, perfectly in sync, downing shots when the waitress offers them, and only concentrating on each other. Maybe we dance for so long because it's easier than talking. The only thing I have to remember is not to kiss her.

After several hours, I don't know where anyone has gone, and I don't care to find out. Instead of going back to the VIP room, I guide Quinn out of the club.

"Jamison, what are you doing? The others will wonder where we are."

"No, they won't. Everyone is involved in their own issues."

"They won't?"

I'm already hailing a cab. "No, doll."

"Where are we going?"

"Back to your place, unless you want to come to Noah's with me?"

"Won't they wonder where you are if you are at my place?"

The cab pulls up, and I open the door. "No one is keeping track of me. Get in."

She gets in, and I follow, crushing my lips into hers the moment I tell the cabbie where to take us.

"It's too much torture not being able to kiss you in public," I say between kisses.

"I know."

"Let's stop pretending, then."

She freezes and pushes her head to mine, closing her eyes.

Crap. What did I say now?

"Doll, what's wrong."

"You're married. All your friends know you are," she whispers.

"Yes, and they know the entire story. No one is going to judge you or us."

She blinks as a tear slips down her cheeks.

I take a deep breath and kiss it. "I'm so sorry I've hurt you. What do I have to do so we can get past this?"

"I don't know. I want to. You don't know how badly I want to move forward, but I don't know how."

Okay. This is progress. At least she's talking to me about it again.

I pull her into my chest and kiss her head. Since we're in a cab, I murmur to her, "Nothing has changed. The only woman I've ever loved is you. We can have a great life together. Move to New York, and we'll figure this out."

She doesn't say anything, and another tear falls, crushing my soul further.

The cab pulls up to her building, and we get out. Saying nothing, we make our way into her apartment, and I lead her over to the couch then guide her onto my lap. "I love you."

"I know you do."

"Do you still love me?" My pulse beats in my neck, scared of what she might say.

"Yes," she whispers.

"I'm so sorry I didn't tell you sooner. If I could turn back time, I would. But I can't change that."

"I know you're sorry. And I believe you. I forgive you for not telling me sooner."

She forgives me?

"You do?"

"Yes. I could have told you what I was doing all those months. Then you wouldn't have questioned my love or commitment to you."

"You didn't do anything wrong. This is all on me."

She bites her lip.

I cup her face. "We can still have a great life together. Move to New York."

"I can't."

"You can."

"Stop pressuring me," she cries out.

I sigh. "You just said you forgive me. Nothing has changed."

"Stop saying that. You're married."

"You know the circumstances."

"Yes, Jamison. I know the details. It doesn't change facts."

"What we have is worth more than paper."

"It's not just a piece of paper."

"It is to me."

"Well it isn't to me."

I'm confused. "Does this mean you're never moving to New York?"

She sighs and quietly says, "No. I'm not saying that."

"Then what are you saying, Quinn?"

"I need to get past it before I can move."

Okay. At least she isn't telling me there's no possibility.

I brush my lips against hers in a quick kiss. "What can I do to help you move past it? How can I show you that it doesn't affect our relationship?"

"I don't know. Give me time."

"How much time?"

"Jamison, I don't know. My entire family hates me right now." Another tear falls.

My gut flips. I'm sick over Quinn being at odds with her mother and brother over us. "They don't hate you. They are upset about me. I'm sorry I've caused trouble between you and your family."

"This isn't easy for me. I love you, but I love my family. I have to figure out how to deal with all this."

I let out some air. "I know it isn't easy for you, and I'm sorry. I'll back off. Just don't give up on us."

She strokes the side of my head. "I'm not. But I need time."

"Okay. I'll give you time."

"Can we go back to having fun tonight? I need a break from all this."

"Yeah, doll. Let me take care of you all night."

21

Quinn

"CHASE IS FREAKING OUT," JAMISON TELLS ME.

"Why?"

"He said Vivian has a date tonight. Noah's suggesting we all go out now. Find out from Vivian what's going on. The last thing I want is to turn our date into a group thing."

I sigh. "I'll find out."

"Are you trying to make Chase jealous?" I text Vivian.

She immediately calls me, and I pick up. "Are you?"

"Hello to you, too." Vivian laughs.

"Sorry. Jamison texted me that Chase told him you have a date tonight?"

"I do."

"With who?"

"Trent."

"Who's that?" I've never heard of him before.

"A guy I've seen a few times."

"So, you aren't trying to make Chase jealous?"

"No. And why would he be jealous when he's got his stash of friends with benefits on the side?"

I laugh. "Because Chase has it bad for you."

Vivian groans. "No, he doesn't. If he had it bad, he would be done with Meredith, and he's not."

"Ms. Thursday?"

"Yep. So are you going out with Jamison tonight?"

"Yes, but don't make a big deal about it to Piper and Charlotte."

"I won't. What's going on with you two?"

I sigh. "Nothing."

"Quinn. I know the whole story, remember?"

No, you really don't know the entire story. "I don't want to talk about it. Have fun on your date."

"Okay. You, too."

I hang up and text Jamison. "Vivian is going out with a guy she's gone on a few dates with."

"Noah just reserved a table at some new bar. He says we're all going out. Piper is going to call you."

"Seriously? Can't we get out of it?"

"Yes, if you let me tell them I'm hanging out with you and only you tonight."

"No, don't. I can't answer questions they will ask, when I don't know the answers myself."

My phone rings. "Hey."

"Quinn, what questions are you so worried about? Why don't we just come up with some answers together, and then we can stop hiding. I don't want to go to a bar tonight with everyone. I had everything planned for our date."

My phone starts beeping, and I'm relieved. "It's Piper. I need to answer this."

"Quinn—"

"I'll call you in a bit." I switch over the line. Sure enough, Piper is inviting me out. I tell her I'll go and text Jamison.

It's not that I don't want to go out with Jamison alone. I do. But I'm not ready to have twenty questions thrown at me about our relationship.

Plus, all of Jamison's friends will know you are his mistress.

"Quinn, how could you go down this path? You know the screwed-up life I live with your father," my mother's voice runs through my head from when she spoke with me one-on-one after my brother stormed out of her birthday dinner.

"Don't refer to him as my father," I said in disgust about the man I've always known as her boss and found out was my father when I was eighteen. "And Jamison isn't Maximillion. He's not cheating on his wife."

She grabbed me by the shoulders. "Men all have their stories. I don't want you ending up like me. I'm trapped. You're not."

"You aren't trapped. You choose to be with him. You choose to continue fucking him behind his wife's back."

"Watch your mouth."

"No. I'm not going to sit here and listen to you be a hypocrite. What you are doing is wrong. You're lying, and your lover is a cheater. I'm not doing anything like that."

She sarcastically laughed. "You think you aren't his second priority? He has a wife. You will always be his second priority."

"I'm not," I say, but in the back of my mind, I can't help but feel like maybe my mom is right. And it scares me.

"Don't be a fool like I am. Leave him now and move on with your life. You are young. You still have a chance for a normal relationship."

"I'm not leaving him. I love him," I told her.

It's the truth. I love Jamison so much it pains me to be away from him. And I know I'm hurting him by not moving to New York and telling our friends that we're together, but I can't figure out how to get past the fact he is married. Sham or not, he is still married.

And you are his mistress.

Shame once again fills me. I wish I could figure out how to not feel this way.

You will figure this out, Quinn. What you have with Jamison is real. Just get ready, have fun tonight, and worry about this tomorrow.

I spend the next hour getting ready. There is a knock on my door. I look out the peephole and see Jamison.

I open the door. "What are you doing here?"

"Everyone is down in the car. I came up so I could steal a kiss." He bends down and kisses me, embracing me tightly to him, making me feel like I am his everything.

But you aren't. He still has his wife to take care of and protect.

I retreat from the kiss. "What did you tell the others?" I ask in a panic.

"Hey, Jamison, thanks for the awesome kiss," he teases me.

I wince at him. "Sorry," then tug him down for another kiss.

He wraps his arms tight around me. "This is more like it," he murmurs between kisses. "And I told them I had to use the restroom so I would come to get you."

"Did they see you punch in my code?"

He sighs. "No. Someone was walking out, and I grabbed the door."

Relieved, I kiss him again and my body throbs against his hardening erection.

"By the way, you look beautiful."

"Thanks. You smell nice." I roll my tongue against his as he caresses my back under my shirt.

"Let's tell them to go without us," he murmurs.

I giggle. "We can't. Let's go."

He groans.

"Sorry. Are you mad I continue to keep this between us?"

He brushes the hair off my face. "No. I'm not mad at you. I'm ready when you are to tell everyone, but it's your call."

"Maybe we can find a dark corner somewhere tonight," I tease him.

"Challenge accepted." He winks then grabs my coat. "Let's go, doll."

He leads me through my building and out to the car. Noah, Piper, and Chase are waiting. Instead of sitting next to Jamison, I take the seat next to Piper.

As soon as the door shuts, Chase asks, "How serious is this between Vivian and this guy?"

I cross my arms. "That's an interesting question coming from you."

"What do you mean?"

"Is it Thursday?" I smirk.

"What does that mean?"

I remember the pact we all made and decide it's best not to say anything further. "Nothing. She's only gone on a few dates. It's not serious yet."

"Yet?" he says in a panic.

"Jeez. Chill out. You're the no-relationship guy, remember?" I tell him.

"She has a good point," Noah says.

"Stop being a hypocrite." Piper glares. "You can't expect Vivian to possibly want to have anything to do with you if you aren't going to commit to her. She's not someone to be played, Chase."

"One, I don't play girls. Two, I would never play Vivian. Three, you don't know anything about my dating life, so stop making assumptions," Chase fires at Piper.

"Can we all cool it?" Jamison asks.

The car parks outside the bar, and Chase flings the door open and gets out. The rest of us follow. Piper and I know the bouncer, and we go right inside.

"What the hell is she doing kissing him?" Chase growls, pointing to Vivian.

"Chase." Jamison puts his hand on his arm. "She's on a date. Calm down. Be smart."

"Let's go to our table," I suggest.

"You can all go." Chase makes a beeline toward Vivian.

"Oh shit," Noah groans. He and Jamison are on Chase's heels, and Piper and I follow him.

"He's such a hypocrite," Piper says.

I sigh and continue dodging people in the crowded bar.

We are all in front of Vivian, who's sitting on Trent's lap, and he's got her on lockdown, kissing her. Jamison and Noah have moved in front of Chase. Piper and I step in front of all of them.

I tap Vivian on the shoulder.

She turns around and yells over the music, "Why are you all together?"

I give her a look not to out my relationship with Jamison. She's been drinking but takes the hint.

"Who's your friend?" Piper asks her.

"Oh, sorry. This is Trent." She turns toward him and points everyone out. "These are my friends, Quinn, Jamison, Piper, Noah, and Chase." She quickly looks away from Chase.

Trent pulls her in closer to him and shakes everyone's hand. When he shakes Chase's, he says, "Whoa. You got quite the grip there."

"Sorry, man, do I?" Chase says innocently.

"We have a table reserved. Come sit with us?" Piper asks.

"That would be great," Trent answers, and Vivian looks slightly panicked.

We all leave to go to the table. When we get there, Trent arrives, but Vivian and Chase are nowhere to be seen.

"Where's Vivian?" Trent asks.

Jamison puts his hand on his back. "I need a drink. You need another?"

"Yes."

The waitress approaches, and, after we order our drinks, Trent orders a round of shots.

After several rounds of shots, and Noah and Jamison keeping Trent occupied, I stand up. "I'm going to go make sure Vivian is okay." I leave and check out the bathroom, but she isn't there. I look across the crowded bar and see another hallway. I push through the crowd and run into Chase and Vivian, coming out of a dark room.

"Where have you been? Trent is looking for you, and the guys are trying to distract him."

"Umm..." Vivian looks at Chase for help.

"I'll go tell Trent you're in the bathroom, and, Quinn, you walk out with Vivian," Chase says.

Chase starts to walk away, and she grabs his arm.

He turns back.

"Thank you for helping."

He winks and walks away.

I put my hand on her arm. "What did you two just do?"

"Don't ask."

"Did you—"

"No. But if you need some privacy with Jamison, that room is a good place." She laughs and winks.

Hmm. That's not a bad idea.

"Hey, why aren't you out with Jamison by yourself?"

"Because of your man."

"Sorry?"

"Chase was sulking, so Noah decided we all were going out, and Jamison couldn't get out of it without telling him he was going out with me, and I didn't want him to do that."

"Why the secrecy, Quinn?"

"I don't want to talk about it. Let's go." Before she can ask me any more questions, I grab her hand and guide her through the bar and to the table.

The next few minutes are chaotic. Trent is wasted. More shots are on the table, and he tries to feed Vivian one. She ends up saying she is sick and ditches us. Chase runs after her, and Trent is left at our table.

Jamison's hand is under the table and on the inside of my thigh, inching up my skirt, creating a heat wave in my panties.

Screw this.

I down my third shot of the night, excuse myself to the bathroom, and go into the room where Vivian was. It looks like a small meeting room.

I take my phone out of my purse and text Jamison. "Go to the back of the bar to the hallway on the left. Fourth door on the right. Come by yourself."

Within minutes, Jamison is inside the room with me. I lock the door.

"Quinn, you okay?" he asks in a worried voice.

I step back against the wall, grab his shirt, and pull him into me. The music is so loud it's vibrating into my back. I lace my hands around his neck and crush my lips against his.

He urgently sticks his tongue in my mouth and presses his body closer to mine. The hardening of his erection jabs against my stomach and his hands slide through my hair.

"I've never done it in a bar," I murmur between kisses.

He groans in my mouth and reaches for his wallet. His lips never leave mine as he fumbles for the condom, finds it, and tosses his wallet on the floor.

I release his pants, and they fall as I shove his boxers along with them.

One song ends and another begins to hum into my body. He picks me up. I wrap my legs around him and move my panties to the side as he enters me in one thrust.

"Oh!" I cry out, not worrying about how loud I am as the music pounds into my ears, and he fills me.

"Fuck, you're tight," he growls, thrusting into me in pace with the music.

I grab his shoulders tighter, leaving no room between him and the wall except for my body.

The buzz of the alcohol, music, and his energy brings heat to my body, scorching all my cells, searing away all my insecurities about us and the issues we have.

"We're so good together," I cry out, as he unleashes a new wave of tingles throughout me.

"We belong together," he grunts.

"I know. We...oh God!" I yell as my first orgasm rages through me, and my high oscillates in every atom.

"That's it, doll," he growls and ferociously presses his lips into mine.

My limbs tighten around him as my toes curl from the ricocheting zings that embody me.

He pushes his head to mine. Through the darkness, I see his green eyes, drilling into mine, looking for my acceptance, pleading for my commitment. "I'm yours, and you're mine."

"Yes," I cry out. It's true. No matter what I do to try and figure things out and make sense of it all, the one clear thing is that I am Jamison's, and I only want him to be mine.

A bead of sweat drips down his cheek.

"I need you, doll."

"I need you."

"I'll give you everything I have. Move to New York," he pants out while thrusting into me harder.

Another orgasm hits me, and my mouth forms into a permanent O as I gasp for breath.

"Tell me you'll move," he commands.

But I can't think. I can't talk. All I can do is groan as my eyes roll and I see stars from the surge of endorphins.

"Fuuuuuck!" he calls out as he pumps hard into me, pushing me into another high.

I'm so spent, my limbs are limp. I'm held up by the wall and him, and my face is buried in his neck.

He stops thrusting and doesn't move as my insides continue to quiver around him. Our chests heave together. When he finally steps back, I release my legs from him.

"You okay to stand, doll?"

"Yes."

"Move to New York. Whatever I have is yours. Come back with me on Sunday."

I sigh. "I can't. I need more time."

Disappointment and pain flood his face.

"I'm sorry."

He nods. "I am, too. Let's get back before the others question where we are."

22

Jamison

The car pulls up in front of Quinn's building.

"I'll walk you up," I tell her.

"I'm okay," she giggles and crawls over my lap. We've all been drinking pretty heavy, more than usual, and it's after two in the morning.

I look at Piper and Noah. "You guys go. I'll grab a cab back."

"We can wait," Piper says.

I look at Noah. "I think I need some air. Go back without me. I've got your penthouse code."

Noah nods, catching my drift. "Sounds good."

Quinn is trying to keep us under wraps, but the guys aren't stupid. They know something is going on. I'm pretty sure Piper and Charlotte do as well, but they haven't said anything to me. I don't say anything to Quinn. I don't want her worrying any more than she already is.

"I'm fine," she giggles again. "I'll see you all later." She puts her finger on my nose seductively before reaching for the car door.

Yep, Quinn's drunk or she wouldn't be touching me in front of Noah and Piper. Not that I'm not feeling some effects of the alcohol.

"I'm going to walk you up." She steps out, and I follow. "See you guys later."

The car takes off. Quinn and I stand in the cold, outside on her front stoop, while she fumbles to punch in the right code.

"Let me help you, doll." I grab her hand and guide her finger to each button.

She giggles some more, turns, and wraps her arms around my neck. "You're sooooooo good to me."

I smile at her and walk with her into the building so she's moving backward as I move forward. "I wish you'd let me be better to you."

She puts her finger on my nose again. "You can be whatever you want to be to me."

"Move to New York and let me be your man."

"You are my man. My only man. And I love you."

I push the elevator button. "That's good because I only love you. Move to New York with me."

The elevator door opens, and I push her to the side wall and push the button.

"You seem to really want me to move." She giggles again.

"I do." I cup her face. "You're torturing me. Come to New York. Let me take care of you."

And she is. Every day that goes by, I long for her to be with me. It's the worst feeling I've ever known, and I'm ready for us to start our life together.

"I should move. You could keep me warm every night."

"Yes, I will," I eagerly say.

The elevator opens, and I quickly guide her to her apartment. "Give me your key, doll."

We get inside. I lock the door and guide her into the bedroom from the glow of the streetlights outside her window. I'm feeling a little wobbly but Quinn's wobblier.

She tears her shirt off, twirls it in the air, and releases it in my direction, giggling.

"If I moved to New York, I could kiss you like this every day." She pulls me down, and we sloppily kiss each other.

I push her skirt off her and release my clothes then pull her onto the bed with me. "If you move to New York, I'll do more than just kiss you every day."

"You would like that, huh?"

My perma-grin is so wide, my cheeks start to hurt. "Guaranteed."

"Do you think I would be a good New Yorker?"

"I think you'd make the best New Yorker. And you could write and do whatever else you wanted."

"Whatever I want?"

I kiss her. "Yes, whatever you want."

She giggles then her face gets serious. "I have a secret to tell you."

I put my face next to hers on the pillow. "Tell me."

"I love you."

"I love you, too."

"I cry myself to sleep most of the time."

My chest tightens. I brush my thumb on her cheek. "Why do you cry, doll?"

"Loving you hurts so bad."

I had lots of drinks, and so has she, but her words pierce my heart.

"Why does loving me hurt, doll?"

Tears fill her blue eyes. "Because I want it all with you, but I can't have it."

"But we can have it all. Move to New York. I'll prove it to you."

"My mother says, 'Never move in with a man unless you have a ring on your finger.'"

Is that what she needs? She needs a ring and then she'll move?

"What would you want your ring to look like, doll?"

"I don't care. I only want to be yours."

"You are mine."

"I don't want to share you."

"You don't have to share me with anyone."

"I have to share you with Valeria. And I want to hate her, but I don't. I like her. What kind of person am I that I actually like your wife?"

I stroke her hair. "You're an amazing person, that's the kind of person you are."

I've never loved or wanted to marry any woman I've dated. I have no doubts about Quinn. If I could marry her, I would.

"I want you as my wife, not Valeria."

"You do?"

"Yes. And if you move to New York, it'll be just like we're married. I'll share everything I have with you. Whatever you need from me, I'll provide. You won't go without anything. We can do whatever we want."

"Whatever we want?" she says sleepily.

"Yes."

She yawns.

I pull her into my arms. "You're tired. Let's go to sleep, doll."

She snuggles into me. "Okay. Just don't ever let me go."

I kiss the top of her head. "You don't have to worry about that, doll."

———

WHEN I WAKE UP, QUINN IS STILL IN MY ARMS. I PULL HER TIGHTER to me, and she stirs.

"Morning, doll."

She closes her eyes. "Ugh. How much did we drink?"

I chuckle. "Too much. I blame the shots."

"I vaguely remember getting out of Noah's car last night."

"You don't remember our conversation?"

She pauses for a moment then puts her hand on her face. "No. But did I strip for you?"

"You only threw your shirt at me."

"Did we have sex?"

"Only at the bar. Please tell me you remember that."

Her face flushes. "I remember that."

"Good. You have permission to pull me into a dark corner of a bar anytime."

She giggles, and my phone rings.

I get out of bed, grab my pants that are on the floor, and pull my phone out of my pocket. Climbing back in bed next to Quinn, I pull her in my arms and answer it.

"Hey, Noah."

"Jamison, we need to run interference with Xander."

"Has Charlotte talked to him yet?"

"No. We're meeting at his hotel around one."

Shit. I wanted to hang out with Quinn all day.

"Hold on a minute." I put the phone against my body so Noah can't hear. "The guys are getting together around one to make sure Xander is okay."

"Go."

I look at the phone. It's ten o'clock. At least I can hang with Quinn for a few hours. "Okay, text me what hotel he's at, and I'll meet you there."

"Want a change of clothes?"

Nope. I already have extra clothes I've left at Quinn's all these months.

I don't say anything about it because Quinn would freak. "I'm good. See you there." I hang up.

"So, Noah knows you stayed here?"

"I'll tell them I slept on the couch if you want."

Quinn bites her lip and scans my eyes nervously.

Great. She's going to have anxiety over me staying the night.

"Don't get upset. They aren't going to judge you. I know what you're worried about, but they would be happy for us."

She strokes my hair. "Actually, I was thinking that maybe it's time to stop hiding. Not tell them but not worry about it so much. If they figure it out, then they figure it out."

I grin at her. "Really?"

She takes a deep breath. "I'm not ready to move to New York yet. But if I am going to, we can't hide, right?"

Yes! Progress!

I shake my head and smile bigger. "No, we can't."

She takes a deep breath. "Then, let's not worry about it anymore."

I lean over on her and cup her face in my hands. "You just made me really happy."

"Yeah?"

"Yeah. I think I'm going to have to give you some extra treats for that."

"You'd better start now. Time's ticking."

I spend the next few hours in bed with Quinn.

I leave to meet up with the guys, and all hell breaks loose in the next few hours.

Charlotte sees Xander and the rest of us sitting in a cafe talking to Xander's ex-Billie. Xander runs out of the restaurant, chasing Charlotte down the street, and she doesn't stop at the crosswalk. A car plows into her. Noah, Chase, and I go into paramedic mode, but we have no equipment and do what we can until the ambulance arrives.

Xander rides with Charlotte in the ambulance, and Noah's driver picks us up.

On the way to the hospital, I call Quinn.

"Hey, doll, where are you?"

"I'm finishing up some errands on the other side of town."

"Can you sit down a minute?" I ask her.

"I'm sitting down in my car. Why?"

Crap, she's driving.

"Can you pull over for a minute?"

Panic laces her voice. "Jamison, what's wrong? You're freaking me out."

"Don't freak. Can you pull over?" I hear the noise of her blinker in the background.

"Okay. I'm in a parking lot. What's going on?"

"I need you to stay calm, okay, doll?"

"Jamison, tell me what is happening."

I take a deep breath. "Charlotte got hit by a car."

"What?" Quinn cries out.

"She ran through a crosswalk."

"What?" she repeats.

"Quinn, tell me where you are, and I'll come get you."

"Jamison, is she alive?" Quinn's voice is shaky.

"Yes. She is. Where are you?"

"On the other side of town."

"I'll come get you."

"No, I'm in my car. I'll meet you at the hospital."

"Stay where you are, and I'll hop in a taxi. I'm just getting to the hospital now."

"I'm already back on the road. I'll meet you there."

"Are you okay to drive?"

"Yes. I'll see you in ten minutes or so."

The car pulls up to the hospital, and Noah and I get out. Chase stays in the vehicle to get Vivian. Noah rushes inside, and I pace outside in the cold, waiting for Quinn.

"Jamison, what are you doing out here?" she calls out, walking across the parking lot.

I run over to her and pull her into my arms. "I'm glad you made it safely."

"I'm okay. How's Charlotte?"

"I don't know. I haven't been inside yet."

"Jamison, how bad was it?"

"They are assessing her. She hit her head and lost consciousness."

Quinn puts her hand over her mouth. I pull her into me again. "Come on, let's go inside and wait."

We spend the rest of the day at the hospital. Charlotte is, thankfully, going to be okay. When it gets close to our flight time, Quinn offers to take Chase and me to the airport.

I sit next to Quinn, holding her hand on the way. When we arrive, she and I step out of the car, and Vivian and Chase stay inside.

I pull her into me and give her a long kiss. "I'm going to miss you."

She hesitates a moment.

I put my hand on her cheek. "What is it, doll?"

"Do you think you could come back Thursday night to take me to Vivian's award gala?"

I will move mountains to make it happen.

I kiss her. "Noah and Piper told me about it, and I was hoping you'd ask me."

Her eyes shine brighter. "You were?"

"Yes. And I should be able to. I just need to verify that I can rearrange something for work. Can I tell you for sure on Monday?"

"Sure."

I kiss her again. "Let me know you got home safe."

"I will. I'm going to dinner with Vivian first."

"Okay, doll. I love you."

"I love you, too. Have a safe flight."

I knock on the window for Chase to get out, give Quinn one more hug, and we go inside the airport.

When I leave Chicago, I'm feeling the most optimistic I've felt about us in months.

And it's clear to me what I need to do to help Quinn feel comfortable moving to New York. And I plan on getting her the best ring that money can buy so she sees I'm 100 percent committed to her.

23

Quinn

"You look amazing," Jamison says, zipping the back of my dress up and brushing his lips on my neck.

I'm wearing an off-the-shoulder, long-sleeved, shimmery gold ball gown. It hugs my body and shows off every curve I have. My long hair is pulled up in a loose bun, and a few loose curls frame my face.

"I'm not letting you out of my sight all night," he murmurs in the curve of my neck.

I straighten his gold bowtie. "You don't disappoint, either." Jamison's tux is the perfect accessory for his rock-hard body.

He dips down and gently kisses me. "We should get going."

I grab my gold clutch, and he escorts me out the door. When we get to the lobby, a private car with driver is waiting for us. Once we're inside, he puts his arm around me, and I lean back into the warm familiarity of his body.

It's been a stressful week. Charlotte is recovering, but my boss is no longer nicknamed Half Dick by the office staff. Nope, he's Full Dick now. And that means my work life is worse than ever, and I've put in twelve-hour days the last three workdays.

Jamison hasn't pressured me to move to New York during any of our conversations this week, which I'm relieved about. With everything going on at work, we've hardly been able to talk much anyway, but when we have, he hasn't brought it up.

For the first time since finding out about his secret marriage, we both seem relaxed. It feels like how things were before I knew about Valeria and him.

We are almost to the gala when Jamison's phone rings. He looks at it. "Sorry, doll. I have to take this."

What is so important that it can't wait?

"Hey, V. I'm almost to the gala with Quinn."

He told Valeria about the gala? I know Jamison and Valeria only have a friendship, but a feeling I don't experience very often fills me. It's jealousy.

She has his lifetime promise. Does she need to take his attention on my night, too?

"I can meet up tomorrow. Just text me the time. I don't have any plans for the day."

No plans? I took the day off work to spend time with him, and he knows it. And what is Valeria doing in Chicago?

"All right. Safe travels. See you tomorrow." Jamison hangs up.

I'm fidgeting with my fingers, twisting and pulling on them, giving myself a pep talk not to let this ruin our night.

Jamison grabs my hands. "You okay, doll?"

I force a smile. "Perfect. What's going on?"

"Valeria and Cindy are in Chicago. Cindy's a photographer, and there is a shoot she's working. They want to meet up with us tomorrow."

My gut drops. *Am I supposed to be friends with your wife now?* While I like Valeria, I have no desire to have it shoved in my face.

"Quinn, is that all right?"

Don't ruin the evening.

I put a smile on my face. "Sure."

Jamison kisses me, and the car pulls up to the curb. The driver opens our door, Jamison gets out and escorts me inside. We spot Noah and Piper talking to Chase, Vivian, and her parents. Xander and Charlotte sneak up behind us, and within a few minutes, the guys head off to get us drinks from the bar.

Vivian's mom points to Jamison at the bar. In her broken English she asks, "Quinn, look good together. You be serious with him?"

I don't know why I lie to her, but I do. Even though I told Jamison the previous week that I wouldn't keep us a secret anymore, I automatically say, "We're just friends."

Her brows furrow. "Oh? Too bad. You make gorgeous babies!"

Vivian's mom is obsessed with having grandbabies right now.

I smile big. *We would have cute kids. Jamison would be a great dad.*

Vivian's mom points at me. "Ah. That smile of love, not only friend."

Heat floods my face. I can't deny it.

"Wedding first. Then babies!" Her eyes sparkle.

No wedding. Babies? They would be illegitimate like me.

I feel like I've been punched in the gut.

My entire life, I've detested the fact that my parents weren't married, and unlike the other kids at school who had their father's name, my brother and I had our mother's.

Steven and I had gone to a private school on scholarships. Almost all the kids had parents together. Those who didn't still had both parents involved in their life. We never knew who our father was, and it was something the rich kids taunted us with. We had been called every name in the book by school kids. Bastard. Illegitimate. Impure. Lovechild. Sinners spawn.

Too many tears were shed over the years. While my brother never cried in front of me, I heard him often enough through the paper-thin walls of our bedrooms, crying himself to sleep.

Shame. Guilt. Embarrassment. They were all constant emotions my brother and I felt, even though the choices of my mother should only be hers.

But they aren't. They are our cross to bear as well. And we paid the price over and over.

I excuse myself and head to the ladies' room. No one else is there. I stare in the mirror.

All I see is my mother.

I love Jamison. My world feels lost and empty without him. He makes me feel alive and cherished. I want to spend every second of the rest of my life with him.

But at what cost?

We will never be married. You can never have kids with him. It's not fair to them.

I close my eyes, breathing in and out, trying to calm the flipping of my gut as reality crashes into me.

Since I can remember, I've wanted a family: a real husband and lots of children.

You will never have it with Jamison. You'll always be the mistress—the second priority after his wife.

When I open my eyes, my reflection somehow seems different than before.

Life is about reality, not the dream, Quinn. You can't have it all.

Someone walks into the bathroom, snapping me out of my thoughts. I wash my hands and dry them, then leave the bathroom.

Jamison is waiting for me in the hall, holding two glasses of champagne. "Hey, doll. Everything okay?"

My heart beats quicker. The love I feel for him is undeniable. It's a power I don't know how to stop. "Yeah. Thanks." I grab the glass and throw half of it back.

Jamison chuckles. "Thirsty?"

"Mm-hmm." I down the rest.

"Quinn, is something wrong?"

"Everything is great. Should we go find the others?"

He hesitates but then says, "Sure." Popping his arm out so I can hold it, he escorts me to the table where everyone has taken a seat. He pulls out my chair so I can sit.

Our bodies are like puzzle pieces that fit together perfectly. *How often do you find the perfect match?*

All the guys I dated before Jamison were puzzle pieces that just didn't fit. But we fit together.

I should just be grateful I found someone who loves me the way he does, who I love back just as much. The other stuff doesn't matter.

Jamison has his arm around me, and I put my hand on his thigh and sink into him further. He kisses the top of my head and winks.

Everything about Jamison makes me feel safe and loved. *Isn't that the most important thing?*

The night progresses. We eat dinner, and Vivian makes her speech. After all the awards are presented, Vivian and Chase come over to our table and hang out with us.

Music starts. "I think it's time we dance, doll," Jamison says in my ear.

He guides me to the dance floor. As he holds me close, I melt into him, knowing we were meant to love each other.

I'm just going to have to make some major sacrifices.

It gets late, and everyone has left besides Noah and Piper. "Ready to get out of here?" Jamison murmurs in my ear.

"Yes."

We say goodbye to Noah and Piper, and, as soon as we get in the car, Jamison's lips are on mine. "I've been dying to kiss you all night."

I pull back from the kiss and cup his face. "I love you."

He brushes the hair that frames my face behind my ear. His green eyes drill into mine. "You're my life, Quinn."

I blink back tears and push any thought of anything except him and his love for me out of my mind. We make out the entire way to my place and all the way into my bedroom.

He turns me and unzips my dress, caressing my shoulders and neck with his lips and warm breath. "I want it all with you, doll."

All. I want it all. And I want it with him.

"Yes," I whisper and blink back tears, knowing we really can't.

He turns me into him. I push his shirt off him then release his pants as his tongue explores my mouth, stealing my breath.

We are unclothed, our warm flesh pressing together, limbs wrapping around the other's body, whispering our love and adoration.

Jamison sits on the edge of the bed, and I straddle him, digging my knees into the mattress, sinking onto him entirely. I whimper from his fullness pushing against my walls.

"You always feel perfect, doll." He holds me so close, stroking my back as I roll my hips against him, moaning in his mouth.

My puckered nipples shimmy against the soft hairs of his chest. Tremors roll from my toes, up to my calves, thighs, torso, and into my head.

"Oh..." I breath as my lip shakes against his cheek.

The sexy raw scent of his skin flares in my nostrils.

"Let me love you forever, Quinn." He tightens his arms around me.

"I want you, too," I whisper, wishing everything could be easy and he could wholly be mine.

The inside of my body violently spasms, clutching him as if it knows that he isn't entirely mine and desperate to keep him. "Jamison," I cry out, spiraling in the safety of his arms.

"I got you, doll," he murmurs as he always does, comforting me, reassuring me, loving me.

I ride him out through my high, and as I start to come down, he grabs my hips, pushing me faster on him, sliding into my G-spot, creating a new adrenaline rush so powerful, I'm humming against him, seeing stars.

His orgasm hits me like a hurricane, and I bury my face into his neck, not sure if he or I am crying louder or shaking harder.

We're breathing hard, still holding each other tight, and he murmurs in my ear, "I have a surprise for you."

I pull my face out of his neck. "What's that?

He kisses me so deeply he starts to get hard in me again. Jamison groans.

I laugh. "I like your surprise."

He chuckles. "That's not it." His lips press against mine some more. "I'm never going to get enough of you."

"I don't want you to."

He pulls back and reaches for the covers. Pulling them back, he says, "Slide in."

I slide under the covers, and he gets up and fumbles through his bag.

Why am I so wet?

Oh shit. We didn't use a condom.

"Oh my God," I cry out, putting my hands on my face.

His head snaps toward me. "What's wrong?"

"The condom," I say.

His eyes widen, and he rushes over to me. "Shit. Quinn, I didn't even think about it."

I hug my knees to my chest and push my head down. Tears start to fall down my face.

"Hey." Jamison strokes my hair.

I pick my face up. "I'm not on the pill. I can't take it."

He pulls me into him. "Okay. It's okay."

"No, it's not. I could end up pregnant," I sob.

Jamison holds me tighter. "Shh. You probably won't, but if you were, we would figure it out."

I jerk my head back. "Figure it out? Our child would be illegitimate."

Jamison's face reddens. "Why would you say such a thing?"

"Because it's true."

"Quinn—"

"No! I grew up my entire life dealing with the ramifications of my mother's choices. I won't do that to an innocent child."

His eyes go to slits. "When are you going to realize I'm not anything like your father? You are not your mother. We are not them."

I avoid replying. "What are you saying, Jamison? That you want to bring kids into this?" I wave my hand between us.

He tilts his head. "I told you I want everything with you. Yes, that includes kids if we decide to have them or if something happens by accident."

Is he living on a different planet?

"How exactly does that work?"

"What do you mean?"

"Should I give you a scenario?" I say sarcastically.

"Yeah, give me a scenario, Quinn," he angrily replies.

"Mistress gets knocked up—"

"Stop calling yourself my mistress."

"Stop denying I am."

He scrubs his face.

"So, mistress gets knocked up. Whose last name do the kids have?"

"If we have kids, they would have my name. I'm their father."

"So, my kids don't have my last name."

"You want them to have your last name?"

"No. I want my kids to have the same name we both have. But that is never going to happen, is it?"

His eyes close, and pain floods his face. When he opens his eyes, he reaches for my hand and drops something smooth but sharp in it, then shuts my hand into a fist and pulls it to his heart. "This is my surprise."

"What is it?"

"It's my promise to you to give you everything. It's a symbol of my love for you. It's to tell the world that you're mine and I'm yours. It's me telling you I want you forever, and whatever I have is yours." His heart is racing fast, beating against his chest cavity.

"What is it?" I whisper.

He releases my fist. "Look."

Time seems to stop. My pulse is beating against my neck. I slowly open my hand to discover a perfect square-cut pink diamond ring. I don't even know how many carats it is. Even in the dark of the night, I see it's magnificence. I've never seen anything like it, and I imagine it's rare.

My mouth goes dry. I look up into Jamison's eyes, not sure what to say.

His voice is quiet, tender, but stern. "You're hung up on the wrong details, doll."

I remain quiet.

"The piece of paper means nothing. We are more than paper. Most people who have it don't have a fraction of what we have. Tell me what you want. You want a wedding? I'll give you one. No one has to know it isn't legal. I'll make a vow to you that actually means something to me. You want kids? We'll be parents and raise them together. You want to be together, just you and me, no one else, forever? That's what it will be. Want something else? Tell me."

I swallow hard, with tears running down my cheeks, my insides quivering.

"Move to New York. I'll put you on everything I own. All my bank accounts. All my real estate and businesses. Anything I have will be ours. Tell me what it's going to take to show you how much I love you and that I'm fully committed to you and only you."

"I don't want your money. I'm not after that," I manage to get out.

He nods. "I know you aren't. But if you move, I'll do it."

"You don't have to do that."

He grabs the ring and slides it over my finger. "I love you, and I'm dying without you. I want you to move to New York because I want you forever. What do I have to do? Tell me."

The weight of the rock sits on my finger as I contemplate all he is saying. I don't know what to tell him to do. What he has just promised me is almost everything I could ever ask for.

Except for the piece of paper that makes it real.

I push the thought out of my mind.

"Okay," I whisper.

He raises his eyebrows. "Okay, what?"

"Okay, I'll move to New York."

"You will?"

More tears stream down my face. "Yes."

He pushes me down on the bed and kisses me, whispering his love for me, promising me the world, declaring his devotion.

And I shut off as best as I can the voice in my head.

24

Jamison

QUINN'S MOVING TO NEW YORK IS THE FIRST THING I THINK WHEN I wake up. I pull her closer into me, kissing her head as happiness surges through me.

She stirs but doesn't open her eyes, moving her hand on my chest. The Harry Winston pink diamond looks beautiful in the morning light on her.

I knew when I saw it that it was for her. It's rare, like Quinn, and was what she needed to understand that we can have it all.

All but the piece of paper I wish I could give her. I want it, too, but I'm not going to let a technicality stop us from being together.

Our love is more than paper.

Now, if only I could get Alejandro off my back.

The last month he's been upping the pressure for me to take over his business. He sent one of his men to my office with a notepad outlining his entities and the values. The note along with it read:

Jamison,

My daughter will not lose her inheritance. You will take over. Here's the fortune you will control.

Alejandro

I REFUSED TO LOOK AT THE PAPERS HE SENT AND WHEN I WOULDN'T, the man responsible for delivering the message to me pushed my head on my desk and told me to read. He wouldn't release me until I agreed and read every last page.

It took an hour. I now had information I didn't want to have. The entities he had acquired illegally, by who knows what means, are vast. However, I was worth at least double.

Regardless, I had no interest in taking anything of his over and called V. She was in town and came over, and that was the night Quinn discovered our marriage.

I called him with Valeria, and we reiterated that I would not be taking over. V told him once again that Santiago was the best choice.

A suitcase, full of cash, was the next delivery I received. Like the last one, it was personally delivered by one of his men. I refused it and was threatened, so I didn't even wait for Valeria and called him directly—something I had never done in the past.

"Jamison, I'm assuming you're calling me to tell me you're ready to start?" he said in his authoritative tone.

"Alejandro, I'm getting tired of this. Stop sending me things. I'm never taking over your businesses. Valeria and I have made ourselves clear."

"It's my daughter's inheritance. You will not deny her."

"I'm hanging up now and sending this back."

"You dare refuse my money?"

"Yes. I do. Now stop harassing me."

The next week, I got the keys to a Ferrari that was waiting on the curb. I could see it out the window when I looked down from my office.

That went back, too.

Quinn kisses my chest, pulling me back into reality. "Penny for your thoughts."

"Morning, doll."

Her beautiful smile lights up her face. "Morning. What are you thinking?"

"How excited I am to start our life together."

She looks at her finger, almost as if she's seeing the ring for the first time. "This is really beautiful, Jamison."

"You're beautiful. Come back with me Sunday night to New York."

"I need to give notice at my work. Plus, I have to pack."

I groan. "I'll hire movers to pack. How much notice are you going to give?"

"I don't know. What do you think is fair? A month?"

"A month? Two weeks is standard."

"I've worked there for nine years. I don't want to leave them shorthanded."

I groan. "Quinn. Is this your way of avoiding the move?"

"What? No. I just want to do the right thing."

"Then give a two-week notice like a normal person, hope they tell you to end earlier, and come start our life together in New York."

"Don't you have it all planned out," she teases me.

"I've been waiting for you for months."

She takes a deep breath. "Okay. I'll give a two-week notice. I want to pack myself though."

"All right. I'll just have the movers transfer the boxes to New York."

"So, we are going to do this, then?" She looks at me hesitantly.

Panic rolls around in my stomach. "Don't tell me you're rethinking things, doll."

"No. It's just a big move."

I nod, relieved. "I know. But I'll be there to make sure you are taken care of."

She laughs. "I bet you will."

My phone rings.

She grabs it off the table, and her face falls as she hands it to me. "It's Valeria."

I answer it. "Hey, V."

"Cindy is caught up at work. Can we meet for a late lunch at three tomorrow?"

"Sure."

"We need to find a place close to her shoot."

"Text the location, and Quinn and I will meet you there."

"Okay, darling. I'll see you tomorrow."

"Bye." I hang up the phone. "Cindy can't get out of work. They want us to meet them tomorrow at three for a late lunch."

Quinn doesn't say anything.

"What's wrong?"

She gets out of bed. "Nothing. I need a shower."

"Are you sure nothing is wrong?"

"Yes." She goes into the bathroom, and I hear the water turn on.

I get out of bed and walk into the bathroom. She's already in the shower, her eyes closed, with water cascading down her body. I step into the shower behind her and scare her.

She gasps. "What are you doing sneaking up on me like that?"

"I think you need some help."

"Is that so?"

"Yep. And I'm not going to miss an inch."

———

QUINN AND I HAVEN'T BEEN APART SINCE I ARRIVED THURSDAY. Besides the gala, it's just been Quinn and me, having fun. It's been perfect.

On Saturday, we get to the restaurant, and Valeria and Cindy are in the back corner booth. It's slightly private, which is good since V is recognized everywhere she goes.

They stand up and give Quinn and I kisses on our cheeks, and we all sit.

Something seems off with Quinn, but I can't put my finger on it.

She's probably just nervous about the move. We spent the cab ride over talking about that, so I figure that is what is wrong.

The waitress pours all of us coffee. Quinn grabs her cup with both hands and takes a sip. When she sets it down, Cindy grabs her hand. "Wow! That's beautiful."

Valeria grabs her hand as well. "Is that an actual pink diamond?"

I beam. "Yep. Rare like my doll."

Quinn's face flushes.

"You did good, darling." Valeria pats my hand.

The waitress comes back and sees the ring. "Ma'am, your ring is beautiful! Is that your engagement ring?"

"Umm…" The red on Quinn's face deepens, and she looks down, not sure how to respond.

"Yes," I say, tightening my arm around her.

"Congratulations. When is the wedding?"

Quinn's lip starts to shake, but I think I'm the only one who notices since her head is still down.

Shit. I never anticipated this.

"I gave it to her recently. We aren't sure yet. Can we order?" I ask the waitress, trying to change the subject.

"Sure."

"I'll have the number two," V says.

"Me, too," Cindy tells the waitress.

"I'll take a number four," I say.

Quinn looks up. "Number three, please." She grabs her coffee and concentrates on it.

We are just going to have to figure out what to say when people ask us these questions. We will get through it.

The waitress writes everything down and leaves.

"You're an editor, Quinn?" Cindy asks.

Quinn replies, "Yes."

"But she's really a writer. She is going to concentrate on launching her fiction books when she gets to New York," I boast.

Quinn's face reddens again.

Valeria's face lights up. "You finally said yes! That's great!"

Quinn stiffens. "It's a big move."

Valeria nods. "I told Jamison to give you time. It's a huge move."

Quinn gives me a look I can't decipher.

"Quinn, what kind of fiction do you write?" Cindy asks.

"Thrillers, mostly. I've dabbled in some other areas."

"When you launch, you'll have to let me know. I love to read."

Quinn smiles at her. "Okay."

"Not to change the subject to bad topics, but, V, we need to get your father under control."

"I called him yesterday and told him to stop. Santiago is more than capable of handling things. This has nothing to do with us."

Quinn looks at me. "What's he doing?"

"Nothing you need to worry about, doll. Just trying to get his way."

Cindy pats Quinn's hand. "It's best if we just stay out of it. Leave Jamison and Valeria to deal with him. Unfortunately, he's the thorn in their marriage that pokes them every now and then."

Quinn shifts in her seat. "Pokes them?"

Seriously, Cindy? Did you have to say that?

"What's he doing?" Quinn asks again.

Valeria and I look at each other. We don't usually tell Cindy what is going on and handle things quietly. I don't want Quinn worrying about this.

"He's just being my father," Valeria quickly states.

"That's the truth," I say.

"Does this have to do with him wanting you to run the business?" Quinn asks.

"How do you know about that?"

"You were talking about it the night I found out about...about..." She points between Valeria and me.

I never thought about what we were talking about that night. I was just worried about trying to figure out how to stop her from hurting and not leave me.

"He wants you to take over the business?" Cindy says, surprised.

Valeria and I both nod.

"In order for me to get my inheritance," Valeria adds.

"What is he doing?" Quinn asks.

"Nothing I can't handle," I say.

Quinn doesn't say anything.

Crap. This is not good.

"Let's change the subject," Valeria suggests.

Quinn stands up. "Excuse me. I need to use the restroom." She walks away.

"She's beautiful, Jamison," Cindy says.

I beam at her and agree.

"My father isn't going to just stop."

"I'm going to go use the restroom. You two talk." Cindy gets up to leave.

"Thanks, darling," Valeria tells her. When Cindy is out of earshot, Valeria continues. "I think we need to figure out why he doesn't want Santiago to run things anymore. I wonder if my mama knows something."

"You told her you don't need the inheritance?"

"Yes. She told my father to forget his promise to her."

"But he isn't?"

"No."

"It makes no sense he's coming after me to run things."

"Something is going on. I don't know what, but we need to figure out his motive."

"How do we do that?"

"We could go to Colombia."

My gut drops. "Go to Colombia?" The last thing I want to do is go back to Colombia. Every trip there had resulted in me wanting to leave before I even arrived.

Valeria holds her hands in the air. "We could talk to him. I could talk to my mama in person and see what she knows."

"I think we are grasping at straws. Going to Colombia puts us in danger. It's on his turf. That's not smart, V."

"What if I go alone?"

I grab her hand with both of mine. "V, do not put yourself in danger."

"But—"

"No. I'm telling you this is not a good idea." I am sure she is contemplating it though. "V, don't."

Quinn clears her throat, looking at V's and my hands. I pull away.

"Sit down, doll."

"I'm not feeling well. I'm going to grab a cab back."

"What's wrong." I'm alarmed.

"Just a headache. I'm sure I'll be fine after I lie down."

"I'll go with you."

"No. Stay. Please."

I put my napkin on the table and start to scoot out of the booth. Quinn puts her hand on my shoulder, and I stop.

"Jamison, stay. It's just a headache. I'll go home and take an ibuprofen and lie down for a while."

Cindy comes back to the booth and sits down next to Valeria.

I put my hand on Quinn's forehead. She doesn't feel warm.

"It's just a headache."

"You haven't eaten," I say.

"I'm not hungry. I just need to lie down."

"Are you sure you don't want me to go with you?"

"Yes. Stay."

I reluctantly agree and kiss her on the cheek. "Text me, so I know you got home okay."

"All right."

"I hope you feel better," Valeria says.

"Yes, me, too," Cindy chimes in.

Quinn leaves.

Valeria asks, "So when is Quinn moving?"

25

Quinn

I LIE TO JAMISON. I DON'T HAVE A HEADACHE. INSTEAD, MY HEART is racing, and I feel like I can't breathe. When I get outside, the cold air hits my lungs, but it doesn't help my beating heart.

The cab drops me off at my apartment, and I go inside and sit down on the couch.

They have secrets.

They are married.

I'm wearing a ring that tells the world we are engaged, and we aren't.

My mother has a similar ring. Sure, it's not a rare pink diamond, but it's big, beautiful, and a statement piece.

My father got it for her. My brother and I call it her mistress ring.

I have become my mother. I am Jamison's mistress.

The shame I felt when the waitress asked if the diamond was my engagement ring was the highest it's ever been.

How many people are going to ask me that?

And he said we were engaged. We aren't. We will never be.

I sit lost in thought as the daylight turns into the darkness of night. My phone rings, snapping me out of my thoughts.

"I didn't realize the time. I'm on my way back. Are you feeling better, or do you want me to tell Xander we aren't coming over?" Jamison asks when I pick up.

Ugh. I forgot Charlotte and Xander are having a game night, and I'm supposed to bring the cheese dip.

"No, I'm okay. I'll meet you downstairs."

"Okay. I'm about ten minutes away."

"See you then." I hang up and collect the ingredients and throw it all in a bag. I put on my coat and am walking out the door when I stop.

I take off the ring and zip it into my coat pocket. I can't handle any questions tonight.

When I get downstairs, I only wait for a few minutes before Jamison's cab arrives. I get in, and he kisses me on the cheek. "Doll, you sure you're okay to go?"

I put on a fake smile. "Yep. Headache is gone."

He scans my eyes. "Everything all right?"

"Yep."

He tilts his head and squints. "You sure?"

"Yes. Please stop asking me."

He licks his lips. "Okay."

We ride in silence and are almost to Charlotte's when he says, "Where is your ring?"

My heart starts racing again. "I took it off."

"I can see that. Want to tell me why?"

"I'm not ready to answer questions."

"Are we back to hiding?"

The cab pulls up to the curb. "No." I jump out and quickly get into the building and to the elevator.

I can feel Jamison's stare. We get to Charlotte's door, and I knock.

"Quinn—"

Xander opens the door.

"Hi, Xander," I say with forced cheer.

"Hi. Come in." He steps back so we can enter, and I shimmy out of my coat. I hightail it over to the kitchen and say hi to Noah, Piper, and Charlotte along the way. Setting the bags on the counter, I start to take all the ingredients for my cheese dip out.

"Want some help?" Piper asks.

"Nope, I've got this." I open the drawer I know Charlotte keeps her apron in and put it on and concentrate on the recipe.

"Quinn, you all right?" Piper asks with concern.

"Fine."

"You sure?"

"Yes, can you stop asking me?" I snap.

"Okay. Sorry."

I exhale. "Sorry. I just want to get this made. Leave me to it."

She walks away.

I'm halfway through my recipe when Vivian comes into the kitchen and hugs me. "Jamison is still in town?"

I avoid her eyes. "Yep."

"Is he staying with you?"

"Nope. He can go back to New York now."

Why did I just tell her he isn't staying with me?

She furrows her brows. "What's going on?"

"Nothing."

"Quinn—"

"I don't want to talk about it." I put on my most cheerful voice and once again make myself smile.

"Okay. I'll drop it," she calmly agrees.

"So you and Chase are together now?"

She's glowing. "Yes."

Movement by the door catches my eyes.

Are you kidding me?

"Why do you have bodyguards? First Piper, now you?" I start to cut up the onion.

"Ms. Thursday is stalking us."

"Stalking you?"

"Yes."

Chase struts into the kitchen. "Hey, Quinn." He kisses me on the cheek and grabs a tortilla chip off the platter then pops it into his mouth.

."Ms. Thursday is stalking Vivian?"

His face falls. He finishes chewing and swallows. "Yes. I didn't know Meredith was crazy."

I snort. "She let you assign her a day of the week. That wasn't a big enough red flag?"

Chase's face turns beet red.

"Quinn—" Vivian starts.

"No. Don't stick up for him now that you're together," I hurl at her.

Life was so much easier when these guys weren't in any of our lives.

"Quinn!" She gapes.

Chase puts his hand on Vivian's arm. "It's okay."

Piper and Charlotte sit down on the barstools on the other side of the kitchen. "What are you all talking about?" Piper asks.

"How Chase put Vivian in danger." I glare at Chase.

"Easy there, Quinn," Piper protests.

Piper is sticking up for Chase? What the hell. Since when does she stick up for him?

"Easy there? Vivian has security guards following her because of some crazy woman, and you're telling me to go easy?" I snarl.

"She has a point," Charlotte mumbles under her breath.

Piper puts her hands in the air. "At least Chase hired protection for her. Noah did the same thing to keep me safe. Everything will be fine with security."

I glare at Piper.

"Jeez, Quinn. You don't have to give Piper the death stare," Vivian tells me.

I snap my head toward Vivian. "This is serious. You could be hurt, or worse."

"She's right," Charlotte quietly says.

"If you're going to say something, Charlotte, then speak up," Vivian tells her.

Noah, Xander, and Jamison walk over to us, all looking confused.

"Everything okay over here?" Jamison asks.

I smirk. "Peachy."

Jamison squints, licks his lips, and shakes his head at me.

"What's going on?" Noah softly asks Piper.

"Quinn and Charlotte are worried about Vivian, and I assured them that everything will be fine. Chase hired security and did the right thing. Ms. Looneytunes Thursday won't be able to get near her." Piper points to Vivian.

Chase's face reddens. "Can you all stop calling her Ms. Thursday?"

"Why? That's what she is."

"Was," Vivian corrects me.

"Sorry. You're Ms. Thursday now," I blurt out.

Just like I'm the mistress.

Vivian whips her head back in shock as Chase says sternly, "No, she's not."

"Quinn, can I talk to you?" Jamison asks.

"Whatever you want to say, you can say it here. Let's just put it out there. Maybe you can write a check with it."

Jamison's eyes widen. A hurt look passes over his face. I blink back tears.

I can't do this anymore. This is destroying me. I can't be the mistress.

But I love him.

I don't know how to live without him anymore.

You need to figure it out. This isn't what you want in life. Nothing will ever change, and you'll always be the mistress.

Untying my apron, I take it off and throw it on the counter. I avoid looking at the others, walk out of the kitchen, grab my coat, and leave.

The dam breaks, and tears fall so quickly I can't see.

I jump into the elevator and run out into the street, hopping in a cab someone is getting out of. I give the driver my address and pull out as Jamison is running out of the building.

I get into my apartment, and within five minutes, Jamison is walking through my door.

He puts his arms around me from behind. "Quinn, what's going on?"

I turn around. "I can't do this anymore."

He holds his breath. "Can't do what?"

I motion between us. "This. Us."

He cups my face. "Don't say that, doll."

I sob. He pulls me into him. "I love you, but I can't do this."

"What's wrong. Tell me so I can fix it," he begs me.

"I'm not your fiancée. I'll never be your wife. I'm always going to be your mistress, and nothing you buy me or say will ever change that," I sob.

He holds me tighter. "Please don't do this. I love you and only you," he quietly says.

Everything comes out. "I know. But you have secrets with your wife. You tell her things. She will always be your number one priority."

"That's not true."

I pull away from him and see tears running down his cheek. "It is. And it should be like that. She's married to you. I'm not."

"You're my number one."

I shake my head. "I'm not."

"You are."

"Then get a divorce."

"I can't, and you know why," he cries out.

Because he has to protect her. He made a vow, twice, to her.

"I love you so much, but you need to leave."

He looks hurt. "Doll, please don't do this."

I reach in my coat and pull out the ring. "This is yours."

"No. It's not. I chose it for you. It's my promise to you," he sternly says as his tear drips onto my cheek.

"You can't promise me something when you have a wife. Maybe I'm the selfish one, but I can't be your mistress."

He cups my cheeks in his hands. "Stop saying that! You've never been and never will be my mistress. I'm not cheating on anyone."

"I need you to leave. If you love me, you'll leave."

He closes his eyes momentarily. When he opens them, he kisses me on the forehead and turns and walks away. As the door shuts, I realize I'm still holding onto the ring.

26

Jamison

Present Day

"STOP! EVERYONE JUST STOP!" QUINN YELLS THROUGH HER TEARS and starts to sob.

I pull her into my arms, blinking back tears, and she allows me to hold her, but only for a moment before spinning and crying out, "Don't. Nothing has changed." She pushes me away, sobbing, and my heart shatters once more.

For the last week, I've been slowly dying without her. Seeing her and having her ignore me was hard enough. Watching her cry is like a knife cutting my heart into pieces.

Piper and Charlotte drag her away, and Piper yells, "The three of you can find another way home," as they pull Quinn into Noah's car.

"Quinn," I yell and start toward the car, but Noah and Xander both grab me.

"Let them go, Jamison," Xander says.

"Damn it," I scream as the car pulls away.

"You going to tell us what's going on now?" Noah asks.

"I love her. I want to spend my life with her. She won't get over that I'm married to Valeria."

"She knows why you can't divorce?" Xander asks.

"Yes, of course. But I'm going to fix that." I pull out my phone.

"What do you mean?" Noah asks.

"I can't live without her. I need to get a divorce. It's time I ended this."

Xander steps in front of me. "What are you going to do, Jamison?"

I order an Uber on my phone to take me to the airport. "What V and I should have done years ago. We're going to take Alejandro down."

"Are you crazy? You'll get killed," Noah cries out.

"If that happens, then at least I died trying. I've amended my trust. If anything happens to me, make sure you transfer everything to Quinn, Noah. The papers are in my safe." Noah has been the executor of my trust for years. I never thought he might need to act in the capacity so soon, but knowing what I'm about to do, he may need to step into that role.

Noah looks at me like I've gone crazy.

"Jamison, think before you do this," Xander pleads with me.

"For fifteen years, all I've done is think. I'm tired of thinking. It's time to act."

The Uber pulls up. "I'll see you guys later."

"Jamison! Don't do this!" Noah calls out.

"I'll call you both when I'm back." I open the door and get in.

"You won't come back," Xander cries.

"It's a price I'm willing to pay." I shut the door and call V, who's still in Chicago with Cindy.

Over the last week, I've spent five hours in New York, changing my trust and making sure Quinn's taken care of if something happens. The other day, Valeria and I discussed the only plan we could come up with to allow us to truly live how we want to.

Divorce.

Not in hiding and with the ones who own our hearts.

And I can't live without Quinn. She deserves to have everything she desires, and I'm going to give it to her or die trying. I'm not going to sit back any longer and let the fear of what Alejandro will do dictate my life.

Valeria is ready to stop hiding as well, so we spent too many hours to count, trying to figure out how to gain our freedom.

"Jamison." Valeria picks up.

"V, did you sort your paperwork?" Over the last week, any joint assets we had we split, so if anything happened to us, they could be quickly transferred to either Quinn or Cindy. Valeria had to sign to amend her trust as well.

"Yes. It's all switched over."

"Good. I'm an hour away from the city. I'll meet you at O'Hare."

"We're doing this, then?"

"Yes. It's time to finish this."

"Okay, darling, I'll book the flights and meet you there."

"See you soon." I hang up the phone.

Within an hour, I'm at the airport and checking in. Valeria has bought us two tickets, and our flight leaves in under an hour. I have my passport in my pocket and wallet. Valeria brings me a small duffel bag, and we say nothing as we pass through security.

Once we are through, Valeria asks me, "Are you sure you want to do this? I can go myself."

I cup her face and meet her eyes. "We got into this together, and we're getting out together. Quinn was right about something."

She tilts her head to the side. "What's that?"

"You're my wife, and you're my priority. I made a vow to you. So, we're in this together. No matter what happens, I'm going to be by your side because that's what I promised you, not once, but twice."

She blinks back tears. "But it's my fault we're in this mess."

"I made a choice. So did you. For better or for worse. Let's get the worse over, come home safe, get divorced, and have our better."

Her lip shakes and her eyes water. "Thank you. I couldn't ask for a better husband." She pulls me into a hug. I don't notice the small crowd that is standing back, snapping photos of us on their phones. The only thing I'm focused on is taking Alejandro down and making sure Valeria and I both come back alive.

Bogotá is the busiest airport in Colombia. The city is in the middle of the country, and it takes us several hours of traveling to get to Buenaventura, once known as Colombia's Deadliest City, that has started to have some revival.

Both Valeria and I know that her father has played his role in the city earning its nickname, and we find no comfort, nor do we let our guard down traveling to it or once we get there.

I know limited Spanish, and I don't know the local dialect. Valeria is fluent and maneuvers us through the negotiations required to get us to her father's compound in Buenaventura on the Pacific Coast. Few people will attempt to drop us off at the doorstep of Alejandro Gómez.

We could have told him we were coming, but Valeria thought we could have more power with a surprise visit. I agreed.

After many hours of traveling, we are both tired, dirty, and hungry. When we get to the compound, dusk is setting in. Upon our arrival, we are escorted into the great room to wait. Alejandro and Mariana, who is Valeria's mother, are informed.

"Valeria," Mariana cries out, with tears in her eyes as she walks quickly into the room.

Valeria rushes to her mother and embraces her, crying as well. It has been over four years since they have seen each other, and I know it's been hard on Valeria.

"Jamison." Her mother pulls me into an embrace. She doesn't speak any English and only says my name, but I know Valeria gets her warmth and good nature from her.

"Valeria," Alejandro's cold voice calls out, and I feel her mother stiffen in my arms.

"Padre," Valeria says in a warm voice, and I'm amazed again at what a good actress she is. Over the last week, I've learned how much Valeria does hate her father. I never thought she liked him, but it's a more deep-seated resentment than I realized.

Put on your acting face, Jamison.

I turn. "Alejandro." I nod at him.

Alejandro pulls back from the hug. "Why did you not tell us you were coming?"

Valeria motions with her hand like it isn't a big deal. "Jamison and I thought we would surprise you for your birthday."

"My birthday isn't for two months."

"Yes, but I might be on the set then, so we thought we would come now since you pointed out we haven't been home in four years."

He looks at us suspiciously.

"Padre, are you not glad we're home?" Valeria asks.

He gazes at me and ignores her question. "Have you come to accept my gift?"

I stare at Alejandro, and my lips turn up just a bit. "I'm sure we can discuss that while I'm here."

An arrogant smile grows on his face. "Good. I'm glad you're coming to your senses."

Valeria's mother says something in Spanish, and she replies, walks over to me, and puts her hand on my back.

"I think we need to get cleaned up and ready for dinner. Don't you?"

"Sounds good."

We're shown into the guest quarters, which is the size of an apartment. When the door shuts, I exhale.

"You did good. Are you going to be okay through dinner?"

"Yes."

"Santiago should be there."

"That's what we need."

"Hopefully, I can talk to Mama alone tonight," Valeria says.

That means I'll be alone with a room full of criminals. Awesome.

You're doing it for Quinn. Stay focused. Don't wuss out.

"I'm going to shower first if you're okay with that?"

"Sure."

I take my bag into the bathroom and shut the door. After I turn the water on, I stand with my hands on the counter, looking in the mirror, reminding myself of all the things I need to get right.

Don't commit to anything.

Give both Alejandro and Santiago enough to think they are both getting their way.

Find out why Alejandro doesn't want Santiago to take over.

It's the puzzle piece that is needed to give Valeria and I our freedom. We don't know why Alejandro has gone cold on Santiago, but if he wants me to take over, he has. We need to find out the reason.

27

Quinn

WHEN I WAKE UP, I'M DISORIENTED AND NOT SURE WHERE I AM. Then I realize I'm at Piper's.

Jamison. The events of the day before come racing to my mind.

The hurt look on his face haunts me, ripping my heart for the millionth time.

I don't know why this has to hurt so bad. Why can't I accept his marriage and the circumstances around it?

I get out of bed and walk out to the main room. Noah and Piper are sitting at the table, drinking coffee, talking in hushed tones.

Guess the guys found a ride.

When I went to sleep, Noah wasn't home yet, and Charlotte was still at Piper's.

"I'm awake. You don't have to whisper anymore," I tell them and walk into the kitchen to get a cup of coffee. "Did Charlotte go home, or is she sleeping?"

"Xander came and got her last night," Noah says.

I need to call into work. I'm a mess.

I set my cup of coffee on the table and grab my phone out of my purse.

My gut drops as I see a message from Jamison. "I love you, doll. I'm going to give you everything you want and deserve. Please don't give up on me. I might not be reachable for a while, just know I'm thinking of you."

I blink back tears but they fall.

Piper sees my tears. "Hey, what's wrong?"

I hand her the phone. "What does that even mean?"

She reads it out loud.

"Shit," Noah mutters.

I snap my head at him. "What does that mean?"

He doesn't say anything but shakes his head in tiny movements.

"Noah, you better start talking." Piper glares.

"It means he went to Colombia to take down Alejandro."

The blood drains from my face, and chills run through my body. "What are you talking about, Noah?"

"He said he can't live without you and is going to get his freedom so he can divorce Valeria."

"What? He'll get killed!"

Noah shuts his eyes then opens them.

"Noah! How could you let him go?" I cry out and push the button to dial Jamison's number.

"Xander and I both tried to stop him. He wouldn't listen."

Jamison's phone goes straight to voice mail.

"Noah, he said Alejandro would cut his eyes out!"

Noah looks away.

"How could you and Xander let him go, Noah?" Piper asks.

"Enough, Piper! You stick your nose in Quinn and Jamison's business, leave us an hour away from home, don't give Jamison an option to explain or tell his side of the story, and you make millions of assumptions. Now you're going to blame Xander and me for Jamison trying to fix this situation so he can get divorced and give Quinn what she wants. I'm done listening to this." Noah stands up and walks out of the room.

Piper's face is red, and she sits back. "Shit. I'm sorry, Quinn."

I go after Noah. "Do you have Valeria's number?"

He turns. "Yes, why?"

"Maybe she has service in Colombia."

"I've already tried. It's going to voicemail."

I put my hand on my face. "God, this is all my fault."

Noah pulls me into him. "No, it's not. I'm sorry I said that. This has been a long time coming."

"What are they going to do?"

Noah shakes his head. "I don't know, but I hope whatever plan they have is foolproof."

———

It's been almost two months since I've seen Jamison. Every magazine on the newsstand, as well as TV gossip program, has pictures of Valeria and Jamison and what looks like an intimate moment at the airport. There is tons of speculation about them both, and the reporters have been digging into each of their lives.

The latest headlines discuss Jamison being a billionaire and list out his companies and whatever real estate properties they could find. The reporters also found out Jamison is married to a Valeria Gómez, and they have now put two and two together.

Everyone wants to know why the couple hid their marriage for so long and where exactly they are hiding out.

Shortly after I found out Jamison left for Colombia, my brother sent me a chain of "I told you so" text messages. I blocked his phone number.

I can hardly concentrate at work, and I've been so distraught, I've thrown up several times over the last few days.

Like a zombie, I'm walking out of work and hear my name.

I turn around and almost don't recognize her.

"Quinn, do you have a minute?" Cindy, Valeria's girlfriend, asks.

"Cindy, what are you doing here?"

She looks like she's been crying. I'm sure I don't look any different.

"I'm sorry to barge into your work. I'm going crazy and need to know if you've heard from them."

I put my hand on her arm. "No, I haven't, but come sit down." I lead her over to a couch in the lobby.

Once we're seated, she starts to cry. "It's been too long."

I take a deep breath. She isn't saying anything that hasn't gone through my mind. "Have you heard from Valeria at all?"

"No. Not since the night she left."

"All I have is this text." I pull up the one Jamison had sent me and show her.

She starts to sob.

I hug her. "Hey. We can't jump to any conclusions. I know—" Throwing my hand over my mouth, I jump up and run to the wastebasket, as nausea overpowers me. Right in the lobby, I throw up.

Cindy is quick on my heels and rubs my back while holding my hair back.

When I finish throwing up, she helps me to the bathroom, and I rinse out my mouth and wash my hands.

"You okay?" She looks concerned.

"I must have the flu. I thought my nerves were making me sick because I feel fine after I throw up, but I don't know."

"Have you been throwing up all day?"

"No, I've thrown up right around this time the last three days."

"And you don't have a fever or anything?"

"No."

She parts her lips then stops.

"What is it?"

"Could you be pregnant?"

"No, Jamison and I—" I throw my hand over my mouth. "Oh, God."

"Have you missed any periods?"

I try to remember my last one. "At least two."

"I've been in town working on a big branding project for the last month. The apartment I'm renting is a block away. Do you want to get a test and see what's going on?"

My heart beats fast. All the things Jamison and I discussed about whether we should have kids or not and what the issues were are on replay in my thoughts. But I no longer care about any of it. All I hear is him telling me that we would raise our kids together. I start to cry.

Cindy pulls me into her arms. "Hey, it'll be okay, no matter what the situation is."

"What if I'm pregnant, and he never comes back?" I cry out.

She strokes my head. "Shh. He's going to come back."

"How do you know?"

She doesn't answer my question.

I cry some more, and when I finally calm down, she says, "Let's go to the store. Do you want me to buy the test?"

"Would you?"

She laughs. "Sure. I've never had to buy one personally, so why not."

I start to laugh.

She puts her arm around my shoulder and leads me out of the bathroom. "Come on, then. Let's find out what is going on."

The store isn't far. We pick out a test and go to her apartment, which is only another block away. "Have you had anything to eat?"

"No."

"Okay. Why don't I make dinner, then?"

I nod. "That would be nice. Thanks."

She hands me a glass of water. "No thanks needed. I think I've been going crazy by myself. I don't know anyone except my work colleagues here, and I can't exactly talk to them about this."

"Sometimes, that is better than everyone knowing your business."

"I can see that. Your friends giving you a hard time over this?"

"No. The crazy part is all my friends are paired up with Jamison's friends."

"Noah, Xander, and Chase?" She smiles at me.

I smile back. "Yes."

"They are all terrific guys. Your friends are lucky."

"You know them well?"

"I wouldn't say well but well enough. Valeria speaks highly of them and has told me a lot of stories."

A wave of guilt rolls through me. "I feel bad that I was jealous of her relationship with Jamison. If I hadn't made such a big deal about their marriage, this wouldn't have happened."

"This isn't your fault. Don't you know I've been after Valeria to get out from under her father's grasp? I've pressured her to get divorced so we could marry for years. Don't take all the credit." She winks.

"Really?"

"Yes. And I've had my moments where I was jealous of her relationship with Jamison. But, over time, I saw how he protects her and cares about her. She thinks the world of him. He saved her from a horrible life. It took me a while, but I realized that few people in the world truly care about you, so I decided I was going to be happy that the person I loved had someone else in their life that was a genuine friend."

"That's a good way to think about it."

"Jamison also would do anything for me and I for him. So I gained another good person in my life."

I rise and grab the pregnancy test kit. "Duty calls."

"Take your time. Do you like ravioli?"

"Yes."

"Okay. I'll start dinner."

I shut the bathroom door, pee on the stick then put the cap back on it.

Two minutes. Two minutes to know if my life is forever changed.

I don't need to look at the stick. My gut is telling me I'm pregnant.

I wash my hands, put the stick on a stack of paper towels, and come back out to the living room.

I set the stack of paper towels on the island and look at Cindy. "You want to do the honors?"

She wipes her hands on a dishtowel and comes to the other side of the island. She picks up the stick. "Do you want to have a boy or a girl?"

28

Jamison

Valeria's head is on my pillow.

"Morning," I say.

She puts her finger over my mouth and her lips to my ear. "We have to leave. Today."

I mouth, "Not ready yet."

"You're getting too far in," she murmurs in my ear.

I close my eyes. I'm in way further than I ever imagined I would be. At this point, I'm starting to understand how a man can sell his soul to the devil.

It's way easier than I ever thought possible.

A little favor here, payment for services there, and voilà, you're knee-deep in a shit show.

And then you don't have to feel the guilt.

While my intentions have not changed, trying to gain Alejandro and Santiago's trust to find out what is going on between them has me doing things I never thought possible.

Two weeks ago, I stood by Alejandro's side while he had his men torture a guy and then cut his finger off. And I stood there and didn't flinch, swallowing bile and praying Alejandro wouldn't see my discomfort.

The prior week, I witnessed a man being beaten for not paying the equivalent of a twenty-dollar bill. More bile, and this time, it was Santiago who stood by my side.

Last night was the kicker. Alejandro stood on one side of me and Santiago on another, while their men dragged a guy on the ground behind a car until he died.

They did it for fun.

They did it for sport.

When I got to our room, I collapsed in the shower, and V stepped in with her clothes on and held me while I wept like a baby.

V's observation that I'm in way over my head is the truth. I struggle to remain the same person and not become the hardened one I have to pretend to be, but I wonder if I am.

There are so many demons fighting within me.

Alejandro hasn't told Santiago he is "grooming" me to take over his reign. V's plan is for Santiago to find out from us and not Alejandro. There is no doubt in my mind that Santiago is eviler than Alejandro.

V and I are playing a dangerous game.

Our bedroom is bugged. We know because she found it while I was in the shower when we first arrived. Our only question is whether it is Alejandro or someone else who is monitoring us.

We play the happily married couple. V and I pretend to have loud sex. We cuddle and kiss around others. I take her for romantic strolls, arms around one another and heads close together so we can talk freely without worrying about being recorded.

During these walks I talk about Quinn, and she talks about Cindy. We want to communicate with them, but it's too risky. Everything is monitored.

The days start to melt together, and I begin to wonder if Quinn will wait for me. My final message to her was vague, and despite having her number in my head, I couldn't call her if I let myself. V and I both knew better and threw out our phones in the Chicago airport. The temptation would have been too high and put Quinn and Cindy at risk.

Chicago. It seems so far away. I wonder how Chase is doing with the expansion. I wonder if Noah has executed the clause in my trust I had put in that if I'm ever missing for more than thirty days to make Quinn a trustee with full power over all the assets on my trust. I wonder if Quinn still loves me as much as I love her.

Does everyone think we are dead, or are they holding out hope?

Hope. I remind myself every day to hold onto it.

We're going on three months. A quarter of an entire year. What is Quinn doing? Is she getting ready for summer? Has she made up with her family? Does she ever read the text I sent her and pull out her ring and remember how I poured my heart out to her when I slid it on her finger?

My thoughts plague me all day and night long, and I know that Valeria struggles with her memories and questions of Cindy.

Valeria has spoken with her mother. They go for walks, and she fills her in on Santiago's desire to run the empire. She overheard Alejandro telling his right-hand man and best friend that he thinks Santiago is trying to take over now and is going behind his back to gain power.

That is all we know, as Alejandro has still not disclosed to me why he wants me to take over for any reason except for Valeria to get her inheritance that he promised her mama she would get.

There are two different scenarios for V and me to earn our freedom. We need to find out who is going to reign. Will Alejandro still be king, or will Santiago knock him off? Whoever it will be, we need to be the one to help them do it, in exchange for our freedom.

I ask Valeria over and over if she is sure she can and wants to take her father down. Every day that passes where she sees him lead terror and destruction is another reminder she detests the man. There is no love or loyalty toward him.

When I look in the mirror, I don't recognize myself. I have a full beard. In some ways, I feel that it allows me to hide my emotions better. I wonder if that is why the other men have them, too.

The men are all Alejandro and Santiago's pawns. V and I try to figure out whose side each man has loyalty to, but it is nearly impossible. We think we are starting to see some alliances but have no proof.

"We need to finish this," I mouth to Valeria.

She murmurs, "They will break you."

I understand what she means. Each day, I break a little more.

I learn how to launder money.

I see how to use physical harm to hurt others.

I get a grasp of how addiction, whether it be for money, drugs, or sex, allows others to hold power over you.

There are things I enjoy, like shooting different types of guns, something I would never have done back in New York. But the thing that scares me is I pretend the targets are either Alejandro or Santiago. With so much death constantly in my face, I wonder if I'm becoming more immune to it. Would I kill if I had the chance?

The naivete I once had regarding all these things is gone. Some days, I feel so far into my role, that I struggle to see how I'm going to go back to running a business and living a normal life.

If I don't get killed first and never get out of this country.

When I do get out, will I be too far gone for Quinn even to recognize me?

I lean into Valeria's ear. "Stay focused."

She takes a deep breath and strokes my beard. Her eyes, laced with worry, fill with tears.

I pull her into me and quietly say, "Freedom. We're close. I need you."

She sniffles and composes herself. We get out of bed and get ready for another day of the unknown.

More time lapses, and I'm starting to lose track: more deaths, more insight into Alejandro's business, more longing to feel Quinn in my arms.

We're hitting close to four months when we finally get lucky. At least we hope we are getting the right intel.

Valeria has made friends with Santiago's wife, Isabella. One day, she pretends to drink with her. Valeria makes a few comments regarding Alejandro, and after several rounds of stiff drinks, Isabella starts singing like a canary about Santiago and his hatred toward his father. Valeria plants enough seeds with Isabella about her hostility toward Alejandro as well, and it isn't long before Santiago is waiting for us during one of our long walks.

In some ways, Santiago looks a lot like Alejandro with his dark, cold eyes that are mostly in slits. His voice is gruff like Alejandro's, and he carries himself like him.

But something tells me that Santiago is more dangerous than Alejandro.

"Why are you here?" Santiago looks at us.

"Visiting. Learning the business to make my father happy," Valeria states.

Santiago gapes. "You're a billionaire?"

How does he know?

He pulls out his phone and pulls up article after article about Valeria and me.

"Does my father know this?" Valeria asks.

Santiago shakes his head. "He's too out of touch with the current ways of the world."

"Why are you showing us this?" I ask.

"You have money. You do not need Alejandro's. You are not cut out for this life. Go back to America. Do not try and take what is rightly mine."

Valeria grabs his arm. "We want nothing of it."

"Then, why are you here?

"Freedom from Alejandro," I tell him.

"Freedom from Alejandro?"

We both nod.

"You have no desire to take over the business?"

"No way."

"Alejandro wants you to instead of me?"

Valeria and I don't say a word. We do not confirm nor deny, knowing we are going down a slippery slope if he is not genuine.

"What would it take for you to leave and never come back? To not attempt to inherit anything of Alejandro's?"

"To be left alone forever from all of this. And my mama to be safe," Valeria says.

"You're willing to take our father down?" Santiago asks Valeria.

"Yes."

"You might get killed," Santiago states.

I put my arm around Valeria and look Santiago in the eye. "That's a risk we're willing to take for our freedom."

29

Quinn

"It's been five months. The clause was for thirty days. You need to sign for this, Quinn. I've let it go longer than I should have." Noah sits across from me in his penthouse and hands me a pen.

A stack of documents with "sign here" stickies stick out everywhere.

"He isn't dead. I'm not giving up on him," I cry out.

Chase puts his arm around me. "We aren't giving up, but decisions need to be made on things."

"I don't want to make decisions. I know nothing about all these things," I tell them.

"We will guide you, but you need to sign, Quinn. Jamison was very clear that he wanted you to have full access to his assets and all the income," Xander softly says.

"He's not dead," I insist.

Chase pulls me into his chest. "No one is saying he is dead. We aren't claiming that. But you need to have the resources to make sure you and the baby are set for life. He wanted that."

"He doesn't know about our baby," I cry out.

"Yes, even more reason that you need to sign. He wanted to make sure you were taken care of, and he would want his child to be," Chase sternly says.

"Stop talking like he's dead." I push out of Chase's arms. "All of you just stop!"

Piper comes over to the table. "Quinn, come sit with us. Take a break." She pulls me up and guides me to the living area where Charlotte and Vivian are.

"I need to go," I tell them.

"Quinn, sit down," Charlotte says.

Vivian pats the seat next to her.

"No. I'm going to go. I'm tired and need to rest."

Piper sighs. "Quinn, you can't leave until you sign those papers."

I glare at her. "I am not signing those papers. Jamison will come home soon."

"His businesses are going to go down if you don't sign. Decisions have to be made. You have to sign," Piper sternly says.

I'm shaking my head no when the bell rings.

"That will be Cindy," Noah says.

"Cindy? Why is she here?"

"Valeria put the same clause in her trust for her. They split all their assets before they left so this could happen," Noah says.

I sit down on the sofa next to Vivian, stunned once again that Jamison did all this before he left.

Why doesn't he come home?

Cindy comes into the penthouse. She walks over, hugs me, and rubs my baby bump. "How's the baby?"

"Doctor said everything is fine."

She smiles at me. "Good. I was worried about you."

The stress of not knowing where Jamison is and what's happening has been a lot to bear. I thought I was going into labor the other night, but it was just Braxton Hicks contractions. Cindy and I were talking on the phone when it happened, and she came over and took me to the hospital. I just had a follow-up with my doctor this week.

Chase walks over to her and kisses her on the cheek. "Cindy, I'm glad you're here. Maybe you can convince Quinn she needs to sign."

Cindy looks at me.

"He's not dead," I softly say.

She turns to Piper. "Is there somewhere private Quinn and I can talk?"

Piper points to the door of their office. "You can use that room."

"Quinn, let's go chat," Cindy says.

I begrudgingly follow her. *I am not signing those documents.*

We get inside the den and shut the door. As soon as we sit on the couch, Cindy pulls out her phone.

"I have something for you that Jamison left."

"I'm sorry. What do you mean?"

"Before Valeria and he left, they told me about the clauses. He recorded something for you. I've not listened to it, but he gave me strict instructions that if Noah said it was time to invoke our clauses, then I needed to give this to you." She hands me her phone, and there is a video with Jamison's face on it.

As soon as I see him, tears start to fall down my face.

"I'm going to leave so you can watch it. I'll be in the other room if you need me."

I stare at his face through my tears for several minutes before I finally hit play. The sound of his voice alone crushes my soul but also fills my heart.

"Hey, doll. If Cindy gave this to you, then Noah is telling you to sign. I know you aren't going to want to, but you need to do it. I don't know what has happened. I may be alive or dead, but I need you to do what Noah says. The guys can help you make decisions if you need them to, but you're more than capable if you want that stress in your life. Otherwise, let them guide you, but you have to sign."

He pauses and stares at the camera for so long, I wonder if the video is frozen. But then tears come to his eyes. "I've done things wrong where you're concerned. I thought I could make up for the fact I was married, but I know now I can't. You deserve everything and not to ever feel like you're my second priority. If I get through this alive, I promise you I will give you everything you deserve and not an ounce less. I love you, doll."

The video ends. I watch it several times and then send it to my phone, my face streaked with tears and my baby bump wet where they fell.

I slowly make my way out to the main room. I walk over to the table. Cindy is signing her forms, and Noah and Chase are still seated. I hand Cindy her phone, sit down next to Chase, grab the pen, and quietly sign my name on all the forms.

When I'm done, Chase doesn't say anything to me but pulls me into his chest, where I silently cry.

———

THE NEXT WEEK, I GET AN ENVELOPE I HAVE TO SIGN FOR. WHEN I open it up, there is another envelope inside. It has my name written on it, and I know it to be Jamison's handwriting.

I debate whether to open it or not, but I finally do.

HEY DOLL,

At this point, you're in charge of all my assets and income. That means you have unlimited resources at your disposal.

Don't feel guilty about spending anything. Quit the job you hate and focus on your writing. Get your books published. The world needs to read them.

I believe in you. You're talented and amazing, and don't ever forget it.

XOXO,

Jamison

PS - Have Vivian find you a place to buy that has security. I want to know you are safe. Don't think twice about what it costs.

. . .

I RE-READ THE LETTER SO MANY TIMES, THE SUN SETS AND THE room becomes dark. When I can't see the writing any longer, I grab my phone.

I text my boss. "I quit."

I text Vivian. "I need you to find an apartment for me to buy with two bedrooms so I have a room for the baby. And it needs security."

30

Jamison

Six months of living in the criminal world and two months of plotting with Santiago, and Valeria and I are ready for this to be over.

We've made a deal with the devil. Santiago wants to reign over Alejandro's empire. If we help to overthrow Alejandro, he has assured us we will earn our freedom.

We just have to get through tonight, and we will be free. I will never have to think about this horrible place again.

It's in my nature to save lives, being a former paramedic, but the destruction I've witnessed over the last six months has me wondering if I'll ever be that person again.

I no longer help people. I watch them suffer. I carry a gun in the back of my pants like a gangster.

Have I become one?

Alejandro has admitted he wants me to take over the empire because Santiago is trying to overthrow him. One of his men who Santiago had confided in told Alejandro and has been acting as a spy.

It's this knowledge we supply that allows Santiago to feed the wrong information to Alejandro.

Alejandro thinks Santiago is going to try and overpower him tonight. He's right. He is. However, what Alejandro doesn't know is that his men are on Santiago's payroll and no longer loyal to him.

At least that is what we believe. Both V and I hope we aren't on the wrong side.

Over the years, Alejandro has not treated his men very well. While Santiago may be darker than Alejandro, he treats his men with respect. It is this aspect that has made the men want to follow Santiago and not Alejandro.

If things go as planned tonight, Valeria and I will walk with our freedom. If one thing goes wrong, we will be in the middle of the crossfire.

"Take this." We are out walking, and I hand Valeria a handgun I stole from Alejandro's supply. "Do you want me to review the safety and other features?"

"I learned to shoot at nine. I've got it."

"Make sure you have this on you tonight. We can't be unprepared."

She stops walking and turns into me. Putting her hand on my shoulder, she says, "You don't have to do this. I can go myself. This is more than you ever signed up for."

"I think we are past that point, don't you?"

"No. You can stay away and not put yourself in any more danger. I don't have a good feeling about this."

"We need to stick to the plan. Deviation creates problems."

"Yes but—"

"Stop. I'm in this with you till the end, remember?"

She lets out a big breath. "Okay."

"Santiago is coming, so put on your confident face."

We review the plan for the evening, and Santiago assures us that he has a car waiting to take Valeria's mama as well as us to Bogotá so we can fly out and never come back.

All Santiago wants is for us to go away and never try to claim any of Alejandro's fortune. He could just kill us, but one thing Santiago has is what he calls "honor." A promise is a promise to him, and he gave us his word that if we were his spies and worked against Alejandro to help him overthrow him, that he would give us our freedom. But if we ever set foot in Colombia again, he will kill us.

Besides our passports and wallets, nothing will go back with us. Not that we brought a lot when we arrived. Valeria has told her mama to make sure she has her passport and any jewelry she wants on her.

We spend the day going through the motions and trying to keep our nerves to ourselves.

Alejandro is plotting with his men to take down Santiago. According to Santiago, the men will turn on Alejandro in a surprise attack.

Both V and I hope that is what happens, or we are toast.

Alejandro has planned a big dinner party. It's Santiago's birthday, and it's his way of shaming him publicly for plotting against him.

It's a formal party, and I've been fitted for a tux, and V's wearing a gold evening gown. It's the color Quinn wore for Vivian's award gala and reminds me we're close to getting what we want. In Valeria's clutch is the pistol I gave her earlier this morning.

The banquet hall in Alejandro's compound has tables and chairs set up for over one hundred men. Men of all levels in his organization have been invited.

Only the top, most trusted advisors, would usually be invited, but Alejandro is planning on sending a message.

Everyone is seated, and Alejandro stands up and invites Santiago to join him. V grabs my hand, knowing that this is the moment we either live or die.

Alejandro speaks in Spanish, so I don't know what he says except for a few words here and there. The women in the room all make a surprised sound, but the men stay quiet.

They all know what is occurring.

Alejandro starts to yell at Santiago, but Santiago is beaming. Alejandro makes a motion for the men to stand up, but only half of them do.

Surprise fills the faces of both Alejandro and Santiago. They each thought more men were on their side.

V's eyes go wide, as do her mama's, and over the next few seconds, screaming and yelling take place, guns are pulled, and bullets are flying everywhere.

I pull V to the floor, under the table, to try and shield us from the shots that are echoing from everywhere. Men start to fall all around us, bleeding and crying out for help.

The paramedic in me wants to try and save them, but V holds me back.

I see an opening to run out of the room. V grabs her gun out of her clutch, and I grab mine as well, and we are about to run when her father lands in front of us.

He reaches out to us, blood gushing out of his chest, begging for help. I am about to help him when V grabs my arm. "No," she says.

Now that Alejandro is at our feet, the path to run is not so clear.

More men fall, and the gunshots become less and less. Eventually, there are no more gunshots.

Alejandro bleeds, reaching for us, but V continues to say, "No," to me.

V and I look at each other, trying to decide if it's safe to move or not when Santiago strolls over to us and kicks Alejandro.

The next few minutes are painful to watch as Santiago inflicts as much pain upon Alejandro as possible. It's only after Alejandro is dead that Santiago puts his head under the table.

He knew we were there.

He wanted us to watch.

"Go. If you ever come back, I'll make sure your death is worse."

I grab V and pull her out from under the table. "Let's go," I tell her.

Only a dozen men are left standing. We're on our way out when we see her mama.

V starts screaming. Her mama is covered in blood, and her eyes are frozen. There is no life left in her.

V throws herself on her mama, speaking and crying in Spanish. Santiago comes over and spits on her mama. I grab V and hold her back as she tries to hurl herself at Santiago.

"Your window to leave is closing," Santiago sneers.

I nod at him and pull V out of the house, pushing her into the waiting car.

The driver says nothing as V sobs about her mama on my chest. The next few hours are a haze.

We stop on the side of the road so we can change and wipe the blood off us with bottles of water and rags that were in the trunk. When we get to Bogotá, the driver hands us one-way tickets Santiago bought.

V is a mess.

"Sweetheart, you have to calm down so we can get through security."

"My mama," she cries out, and I pull her into my arms again. "I know. I'm so sorry. But we have to go. Cindy is waiting for you, and we can't do anything about your mama."

"Cindy?" she says as if she forgot about her.

I stroke her hair. "Yes. She's waiting for you. I need you to pretend you're in a movie right now. You're going on vacation. Can you do that?"

She takes a deep breath and nods.

"Good. Let's get through security and go home."

"Home?"

I brush her hair off her face. "Yes. Home."

She sniffles and pulls herself together. "Okay."

We make it through security and onto the plane. Halfway through our flight, V finally comes out of her shock. "Do you think they waited for us?"

"I don't know, but I'll die if she didn't."

31

Quinn

EVERY DAY THAT PASSES IS ANOTHER STAB TO MY HEART. I MISS SO
many things he did that I took for granted.

The way he would kiss the top of my forehead, or the safe feeling
I had when he held me in his arms, or how he would carry my
bag for me.

Small things.

But things that made him who he was.

Is. Who he is. I have to keep reminding myself that he is still out
there.

I've moved into a secure building like Jamison wanted me to and
added him to my full-access list, but I'm scared about so many
things.

In three months, I'm going to be a mother. I don't know what I'm having. I don't want to know the sex until Jamison comes back. So I decorated the nursery in neutral colors.

I've been focusing on my writing, and my first book is about to be published. I don't know what to expect, but it's what Jamison wanted me to do.

At night, when I close my eyes, the biggest thing I'm scared about comes flying at me so fast, I feel suffocated. It's that he won't come home.

I no longer have any contact with my family. When I told my mother I was pregnant, she began to lecture me about how I've turned into her.

I won't have anyone shame my baby or my relationship with Jamison. I see how wrong I was about so many things. Unimportant things I made critical to our relationship when it didn't matter. Jamison said we had more than paper, and he was right. I kick myself daily that I couldn't see it. The only thing that matters is how much we loved each other.

Love. How much we still love each other.

I started wearing the pink diamond ring Jamison gave me a few months ago. I woke up in the middle of the night, dreaming of his declaration to me, and I pulled it out of my jewelry box.

Why couldn't I have just accepted things?

I've tried to stay active and keep my mind off thinking of what he may be going through. Yoga has been my saving grace. I get done with my class, roll up my mat, and put my shoes on. At home, I unlock the door to my apartment and freeze.

Am I seeing things?

It looks like Jamison, but is it? He has a full beard, his hair is longer, and skin dark with a tan, and tears fill his eyes.

I put my hand over my mouth and drop my yoga mat and bag on the floor. He takes a few steps forward and wraps me in his arms.

"Oh my God, is it really you?" I cry.

"Yes, doll, it's me."

I snuggle into his arms and chest like a blanket, feeling the safety I've missed all these months. I look up and tug his head down to me, crushing my lips against him, burying myself in the world I was scared I had lost forever.

I pull back and cup his face in my hands. "Are you okay?"

He starts to sob. "Shh," I try to soothe him as more tears fall down my cheeks.

What has he been through? What has he seen?

I pull him tighter to me, wishing I could take away all his pain.

"Tell me I haven't lost you, doll," he sobs.

"I'm yours. No matter what. I'm yours for life," I promise him. The baby kicks. My stomach is against him, and Jamison jumps back.

"What was that?" he asks.

I cup his face. "That's your baby."

His eyebrow rises. "My what?"

"Your baby."

He steps back. "Quinn, you're pregnant?"

He puts his hand on my stomach. "We're having a baby?"

"Yes."

He picks me up and twirls me around. When he sets me down, he kisses me so deeply, I'm breathless.

"How far along are you?"

"Six months."

"Are we having a boy or a girl?"

"I don't know. I waited for you."

"You waited for me?"

"Yes."

Jamison kisses me again then scoops me up and carries me to the bedroom. Within seconds, our clothes are off and his heavenly lips and tongue are all over my body. Pausing on my stomach, he kisses it several times, tears dampening my skin.

I glide my hands through his hair.

He moves to my thighs, kissing each one then guiding my legs over his shoulders. His tongue dips in and out of my hole then swipes all through my wet folds, slowly, then with more urgency.

"Jamison," I cry out, gripping his hair tight, and pushing his head harder into me as my toes curl and an ocean of flutters roll all over me.

He latches onto my clit, sucking me, flicking me with his tongue, drawing me more into his mouth.

I explode against him, crying out in my high, shaking as only he has ever been able to make me.

Making his way up my body, he spends time on my sensitive breasts, and volts run through me once more.

I want him. Needing him more than anything I've ever needed.

"I missed you so much," I cry out, as tears run down my face.

He cries, too. "All I dreamed about was you, doll. You kept me sane."

Our tongues roll together, my orgasm fresh on his mouth and my limbs wrapped around him.

He flips me over, and I sink onto him. The deep, throaty groan I'd played over and over in my head all these months vibrates against my mouth as his girth pushes against my walls.

"Oh, doll," he breaths .

My body accepts all of him and I moan, circling my hips, as his arms wrap tighter around me.

"We're still perfect together," he murmurs.

"Yes...we...," I whisper, flying into another orgasm, quivering with his hands caressing my back and ass.

"That's it, doll." He stares into my eyes, his warm breath panting into mine.

Rough hands grab my hips and rock me harder and faster into his thrusts.

Our skin glistens with sweat, sliding against the other, radiating heat from every cell possible.

"Oh God, Jamison!" I cry out as he glides along my G-spot and pushes me into another orgasm.

"I got you, doll," he mumbles, kissing me through the rush of adrenaline before he swells inside me, groaning, and pumping his seed hard into me.

As we violently tremble together, he wraps his arms tight around me, and I'm home. That's what Jamison is. He's everything I've ever wanted and more. And I'll never doubt his love for me again or question whether what we have is right or wrong. What we have is so much more than paper.

EPILOGUE

One Year Later

"ARE YOU READY FOR THIS?" CHASE BEAMS.

I grin back at him. "I've never been more ready for anything in my life."

He pats me on the back, and we both turn. There are only fifty guests in attendance. My immediate family, Quinn's immediate family, and our closest friends, including Valeria and Cindy.

And our baby girl, Hope. When she was born, Quinn said, "Hope. Neither of us gave up hope. Let's name her that."

My mom and Quinn's are sitting next to each other and taking turns holding her.

A month before the baby was born, Quinn and I got together with her mom and brother. Things were still a little awkward, but once Hope was born, it seemed like she melted any issues away.

Steven actually is a good guy and we've finally made our peace.

Quinn published her first book shortly after I came back. The dedication read,

To Jamison,

Without your belief in me, my dream would never have come true. But it's not only about this book. You're my biggest dream come true because we are more than paper.

XOXO forever,

Quinn

Her novel has been a huge hit, and she's published several over the last year. I never doubted anything different would happen, but Quinn's confidence as an author has grown, and I couldn't be prouder of her.

When I got back, the paparazzi wouldn't leave Valeria and I alone. After several months, we had a press conference announcing our divorce, and Valeria told the world that she was a lesbian. She and Cindy got married the following month and both are actively involved in gay rights now. The press stopped hounding me and turned its attention on them.

The music starts to play, and Piper, Charlotte, and Vivian walk down the aisle. Noah and Xander are behind Chase with me.

At the first notes of "Here Comes the Bride," everyone stands and turns.

Quinn appears, in a white formfitting dress, with a long veil over her strawberry blonde hair. She's shimmering in the sunlight, and her eyes glisten. My heart pounds, and I wipe at the tear falling.

Hospitals, weddings, and funerals, I don't stand a chance at. Quinn's voice from the first day echoes through my mind, and I chuckle at the memory.

Apparently neither of us do, doll.

Steven walks her down the aisle. Our eyes never leave each other's.

"I love you so much," I mouth to her.

She blinks back more tears.

When they reach me, I cup her face and kiss her. I didn't plan on it, and isn't the normal way weddings go, but Quinn and my journey hasn't been normal. We decided when I returned that we were going to throw notions of normal out the window and always do what we felt was best for each other...for us. And we were never again going to worry about what anyone else thought.

She parts her lips for me, and I roll my tongue against hers as she grabs my head and deepens our kiss. I hardly hear the hoots and hollers of our guests. When I pull back from it, I push my forehead to hers. "You're stunning, doll," I murmur to her.

"So are you," she whispers.

The official clears his throat. "Should we get started?"

We smile at each other and turn, my arm around her waist, my other hand in hers with her pink ring sparkling in the sunlight.

The officiant starts the ceremony, and it comes time for our vows. We have written our own, unlike my previous two weddings where everything was canned.

I take Quinn's hands in mine and stare at her beautiful blue, tear-filled eyes. "Quinn, I give you my vow that you'll always be my number one priority and I'll love you above all else, more than paper."

She nods. "Jamison, I give you my vow, that you'll always be my number one priority and I'll love you above all else, more than paper."

There is nothing else we need to say to each other. Till death do us part is not even a question.

Ready to find out why Quinn's brother Steven was such a jerk? Need a super steamy read that will change your opinion of him? Read The Groomsman Billionaire- click here!

THE GROOMSMAN BILLIONAIRE
BLURB

IT'S COMPLICATED - BOOK FIVE

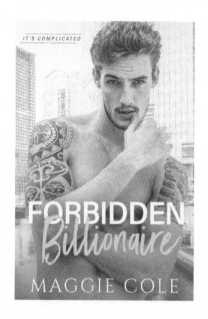

My wedding hookup with my sister-in-law's brother should have been a rebound.

I should have listened to his exes.

A slow burn of adrenaline that will keep you buzzing until you can't handle it anymore...

Worth the wait...

An animal under the sheets...

That's what they claimed about Steven Sinclair on national T.V.

He's super successful, scheduled, and has rules about dating.

I'm only in Chicago for the wedding and to watch my niece for the week...but now he's staying with

me too.

The aching is too much...the heat too hot...the craving on the cusp of exploding...

But his father's sins have consequences in Steven's life.

And that means mine as well.

Read Forbidden Billionaire - click here.

THE GROOMSMAN BILLIONAIRE - PROLOGUE SNEAK PEEK

Steven

MY SISTER, QUINN, AND I ATTENDED A PRIVATE SCHOOL, AND religion class was mandatory. Every day, the teacher would tell us to pull out our Bibles, and students were chosen to write new excerpts on the blackboard. Over one hundred verses exist about the sins of the father, not to mention the countless others on "bastards," children born from "forbidden unions," and "illegitimate offspring." And they all contradict each other. Some say children do pay for their parents' sins. Others say they don't.

From personal experience, I'd say the sins of the father screw with your head and life, and there is no way to escape them. It's like putting a plastic bag over your head and trying to breathe. It's impossible, and eventually, you suffocate.

It molds and shapes you and makes you hold yourself to higher standards and question every move you make. And others don't understand why you make the choices you do or why you try to protect them. All they see you as is a heartless prick.

So, yeah, I believe you pay for the sins of your father.

I remember the first time my classmates put two and two together. They were all from wealthy families. I was the poor kid on a scholarship who lived in the neighborhood they never visited. Their parents may have been divorced or unhappily married, but they knew who their fathers were, so in their eyes, and mine, too, they were better than me.

I only had faded memories from my birth to age four. Then he just disappeared one day. I wasn't enough for him to want to stay in the picture.

Quinn had no clue what he looked like. She was only six months old when he left. I didn't know his name, only *Daddy*.

Whether the teachers did it knowingly or not, every single time one of those verses came up in class, I would be called upon to go to the front of the room and scribble it out. During recess, the kids would recite what I wrote, further driving the heartache I felt about not having a father and isolating me more.

My mother worked several jobs until I was in high school. One day, she came home and announced she became a personal assistant for Maximillion Evinrude.

I remember how her face lit up, talking about her new career and all the ways we were going to be better off.

We were getting an upgrade.

Bye-bye to multiple jobs and having to wear shoes with your toe sticking out until enough money was saved—which happened a lot since my feet wouldn't stop growing.

Hello to designer gifts for my mother and home-cooked meals instead of the typical SpaghettiOs or mac 'n cheese I typically fed Quinn.

But what also changed was my mother's personality. In the past, she may have worked long hours and not been home to tuck us in every night, but when she wasn't working, her world was us, and she didn't seem sad.

At least, that's what I remember. Looking back, maybe she hid it all those years. But once Maximillion Evinrude hired her, her mood would change like Jekyll and Hyde.

In the first year she worked for him, I caught my mother crying too many times to count. I'd see her beaming and in la-la land one day then demolishing a box of tissues the next. And within a week, she'd have a new purse, or piece of jewelry, or a pair of thousand-dollar shoes.

I didn't understand it. Weren't things easier now with her new career? Plus, Quinn and I did everything we could not to cause her any trouble.

When I was ten, my mother sat me down and said, "You're the man of the house, Steven. I need you to act like it and take care of your sister at school and when I'm at work." So I made sure Quinn and I did our homework and were ready for tests. We kept the house clean, got groceries when needed, and went to bed on time. And when my mother said, "You need to keep the boys away from your sister. She's beautiful and a dreamer. She doesn't need to be taken advantage of and ruin her life," I took it seriously. No guy was going to harm her under my watch.

In my sophomore year of high school, going into the second year of my mother's new career, I saw a picture in the paper of Maximillion Evinrude. He was running for governor, and at that moment, everything became clear.

I should have known what he looked like. He had an acting career in California. He might have been a one-hit wonder, but it seemed as though everyone on earth had heard of him, except for

Quinn and me. Whether my mother kept us away from him for her own self-preservation or ours, I'll never know, but I hadn't even heard of him until she announced her new career.

I used to call him *Daddy*. I may have only been four when he deserted us, but I dreamed of him and all the things we used to do before he abandoned us. Once I found out who he really was, I spent hours researching him and staring in disbelief at his family's photos.

They were all over the internet. And the family he claimed as his looked happy. His trophy wife, three kids, and even dog, were picture-perfect.

So much rage built within me, I punched a wall and had to get a cast on my hand. When my mother asked me how I could do something like that, I confronted her. And that's when it all came out.

She was his mistress and never knew it until he decided to up and leave for California to develop his acting career. For almost a decade, he let my mother struggle as a single parent. She fought to keep food on the table and clothes on our backs and still made sure we had a good education. She was determined we wouldn't end up stuck in poverty and always said, "Continue to get good grades so you can get a high-paying job and not end up working three jobs like me."

My father never sent her a dime for our support, and she never took him to court to get anything.

What didn't make sense is he had money. He chose not to help her or us. And the moment he came back into town, she fell back into her role as his mistress. Except this time, there isn't anything hidden under the rug. She's fully aware of her position in his life and that she'll always be the mistress. And for the last twenty years, it's stayed that way.

My mother knows it's wrong. She drills it into Quinn and my heads. But she won't leave him. She says she can't break away because she loves him.

And I don't understand how any woman can love a man who's done what he has and continue to give herself to him, day in and day out, knowing he's going home to someone he chooses other than her.

I confronted him once and told him to leave my mother alone. That only resulted in my mother staying with him for a week.

And when I graduated from college as valedictorian, the job market was shaky. No matter how much I excelled, I didn't know the right people in the right places.

My mother worked her magic on him, and one day, he paid me a surprise visit.

His friend owned a national insurance company, and there was an opening in the finance department. It was entry-level, and I would have to interview, but he could arrange it.

At first, I told him no. I didn't want anything from him. But that night, Quinn got her acceptance letter to college and wasn't sure how she was going to pay for it. I opened all my mail, and several student loan payments were due.

So I caved. Over the years, I worked my way up the ladder and am their youngest VP ever, but no matter how much I tell myself I earned my position, I'll never forgive myself for letting Maximillion help me.

Nor does he let me forget it.

And every relationship I attempt never lasts. I question every move I make. I don't want to disrespect any woman or treat her in any capacity my father would. So I hesitate when I shouldn't and say all the wrong things.

But I also don't trust love. It's what my mother claims makes her his doormat, and if love is so powerful, it'll make you lose your self-respect, then I don't want any part of it.

At least, that's what I tell myself. But then I lay down to go to sleep and close my eyes. And the one thing you can't do is lie to yourself.

To get through the loneliness, I tell myself I just haven't found the right girl. But the voice in my head says, *If your own father doesn't love you, how can anyone else?*

Read Forbidden Billionaire - click here!

ALL IN BOXSET

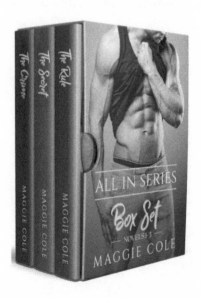

Three page-turning, interconnected stand-alone romance novels with HEA's!! Get ready to fall in love with the characters. Billionaires. Professional athletes. New York City. Twist, turns, and danger lurking everywhere. The only option for these couples is to go ALL IN...with a little help from their friends. EXTRA STEAM INCLUDED!

Grab it now! READ FREE IN KINDLE UNLIMITED!

CAN I ASK YOU A HUGE FAVOR?

Would you be willing to leave me a review?

I would be forever grateful as one positive review on Amazon is like buying the book a hundred times! Reader support is the lifeblood for Indie authors and provides us the feedback we need to give readers what they want in future stories!

Your positive review means the world to me! So thank you from the bottom of my heart!

CLICK TO REVIEW

MORE BY MAGGIE COLE

It's Complicated Series (Series Two - Chicago Billionaires)

My Boss the Billionaire - Book One

Forgotten by the Billionaire - Book Two

My Friend the Billionaire - Book Three

Forbidden Billionaire - Book Four

The Groomsman Billionaire - Book Five

Secret Mafia Billionaire - Book Six

Mafia Wars New York - A Dark Mafia Series (Series Six)

Toxic (Dante's Story) - Book One

Immoral (Gianni's Story) - Book Two

Crazed (Massimo's Story) - Book Three

Carnal (Tristano's Story) - Book Four

Flawed (Luca's Story) - Book Five

Mafia Wars - A Dark Mafia Series (Series Five)

Ruthless Stranger (Maksim's Story) - Book One

Broken Fighter (Boris's Story) - Book Two

Cruel Enforcer (Sergey's Story) - Book Three

Vicious Protector (Adrian's Story) - Book Four

Savage Tracker (Obrecht's Story) - Book Five

Unchosen Ruler (Liam's Story) - Book Six

Perfect Sinner (Nolan's Story) - Book Seven

Brutal Defender (Killian's Story) - Book Eight

Deviant Hacker (Declan's Story) - Book Nine

Relentless Hunter (Finn's Story) - Book Ten

Behind Closed Doors (Series Four - Former Military Now International Rescue Alpha Studs)

Depths of Destruction - Book One

Marks of Rebellion - Book Two

Haze of Obedience - Book Three

Cavern of Silence - Book Four

Stains of Desire - Book Five

Risks of Temptation - Book Six

Together We Stand Series (Series Three - Family Saga)

Kiss of Redemption- Book One

Sins of Justice - Book Two

Acts of Manipulation - Book Three

Web of Betrayal - Book Four

Masks of Devotion - Book Five

Roots of Vengeance - Book Six

All In Series (Series One - New York Billionaires)

The Rule - Book One

The Secret - Book Two

The Crime - Book Three

The Lie - Book Four

The Trap - Book Five

The Gamble - Book Six

Stand Alone Christmas Novella

Judge Me Not

ABOUT THE AUTHOR

Amazon Bestselling Author

Maggie Cole is committed to bringing her readers alphalicious book boyfriends. She's an international bestselling author and has been called the "literary master of steamy romance." Her books are full of raw emotion, suspense, and will always keep you wanting more. She is a masterful storyteller of contemporary romance and loves writing about broken people who rise above the ashes.

Maggie lives in Florida with her son. She loves sunshine, anything to do with water, and everything naughty.

Her current series were written in the order below:

- All In

- It's Complicated (Together We Stand (Brooks Family Saga - read in order)
- Behind Closed Doors (Read in order)
- Mafia Wars
- Mafia Wars New York

Maggie Cole's Newsletter
Sign up here!

Hang Out with Maggie in Her Reader Group
Maggie Cole's Romance Addicts

Follow for Giveaways
Facebook Maggie Cole

Instagram
@maggiecoleauthor

Complete Works on Amazon
Follow Maggie's Amazon Author Page

Book Trailers
Follow Maggie on YouTube

Are you a Blogger and want to join my ARC team?
Signup now!

Feedback or suggestions?
Email: authormaggiecole@gmail.com